Benjamin F. Taylor

Summer-Savory

gleaned from rural nooks in pleasant weather

Benjamin F. Taylor

Summer-Savory
gleaned from rural nooks in pleasant weather

ISBN/EAN: 9783337314309

Printed in Europe, USA, Canada, Australia, Japan

Cover: Foto ©Andreas Hilbeck / pixelio.de

More available books at **www.hansebooks.com**

SUMMER-SAVORY,

GLEANED FROM RURAL NOOKS

IN PLEASANT WEATHER.

BY

BENJ. F. TAYLOR, LL.D.,

AUTHOR OF "THE WORLD ON WHEELS," "BETWEEN THE GATES,"
"SONGS OF YESTERDAY," ETC.

CHICAGO:
S. C. GRIGGS AND COMPANY.
1879.

"ON THE STILE."

SAGE, Caraway, Summer-Savory, and Dill, are four aromatic memories of the old fire-side and garden-side. They suggest the fragrant little trifles that enrich life beyond silver and gold. They are good, winter and summer.

For these records of gypsy-like rambles in sunny days I have picked a leaf from the garden border close to the hollyhocks, and chosen a name — SUMMER-SAVORY. Let us hope the next leaf gathered will not be from among the poppies. That's for forgetfulness.

It is an art to set back the old clock and be a child again. Imagination can easily see the boy a man, but how hard for it to see the man a child; and whoever learns to glide back into that rosy time when he did not know that thorns are under the roses, or that clouds will return after the rain; when he thought a tear can no more stain a cheek than a drop of rain a flower; when he fancied life had no disguises, and hope no blight at all, has come as near as anybody in the world to discovering the North-west Passage to an earthly Paradise.

CONTENTS.

SUMMER-SAVORY,

GLEANED FROM RURAL NOOKS IN PLEASANT WEATHER.

CHAPTER I.

"A HEATED TERM."

THE world is out of sight. The high tides of midsummer have rolled over it. The green volumes of the maples, the tumbling fountains of the willows, the pensile spray of the elms, the golden calms of the ripe grain, the chopping seas of the swath-ridged meadows, have submerged and washed our brown planet quite away. The armed squadrons of corn are marching to the tune of 100° in the shade. They have whipped out all their swords and thrown away the scabbards. Their green knapsacks are growing plump with rations of samp, hasty-pudding and Indian bread. The sweet whispers of the lilacs, telling of days that are no more, have died out of the year of grace. The first flush of June roses has faded, the first love-songs of birds have been sung, the broad zone of the matron has succeeded to the slender sash of the maid, and the year is marching on. It is a splendid tramp, besides being a trump. The white star-blossom of the strawberry has heralded the sweet red Mars of the ripened fruit—the star is a pleiad and the planet has — gone down! There is a faint smell of new apples in the air, that is better than gales from Araby the Blest. There is a suspicion of caraway, and a hint of dill, and a breath from the red clover. Nature is rich in compensations, and her losses and her gains are paired like the embarking menagerie of the first Admiral, when the Ark put to sea with the greatest and only show on earth, bound for Ararat and a market.

The lights and shades of the year touch and tint and change everything but the English sparrow,—that goes right on with its saucy talk and its perpetual fight and its ceaseless paternosters of beaded eggs the year round. Snow or glow, zephyr or northeaster, it is all the same. What a pugnacious, aggressive ounce of British bird it is! It routs our robins and persecutes our goldfinches, and the gypsy baskets of the orioles swing empty. Oh, for another Bunker Hill! And yet some cry, Spare, oh, the sparrow!

100°.

I have been seeking a cool place. The ambition of the mercury wearies me. The thought of Dr. Kane's chronometer, that was so cold it *burned* him, is no comfort. Even the "Exiles of Siberia" are selfish as oysters. There they are to-day, comfortably freezing their feet, and do not offer us so much as a chill of a chance to frost a finger. The little arrow that swings from the top of the barn seems to be welded to the

spire by the solar force, and to be drawing fire with
its barbed point out of the fierce south. The leaves
of a tree by my window curl in the sun, as if they
were trying to get back into the bud again, and be
cozy and cool as they were when the world went
Maying.

The robins sit on the cherry-tree with bills apart
like a V, and their wings at trail arms. I can almost
detect the smell of burned feathers. A match on the
window-sill sets off of its own accord, and commits
suicide to get out of its misery.

Lawyers' clients grow irritable, and desire to
"sue" somebody right away, and talk in a salaman-
derish style about making the defendant "sweat."
Doctors' patients languish and wilt. Heat expands
most things but sermons,—they shrink from an hour
to twenty minutes, and sometimes the preachers
themselves are scorched out of their pulpits, and
flee to the mountains and the islands of the sea.
Some cynic has growled because clergymen take a
vacation in summer, and sneered with an unanswer-
able air, "Are not immortal souls as precious in dog-
days as in December?" As if, with thermometers
at a hundred in the shade, a preacher cannot safely
leave his flock so long as he leaves the orthodox
suggestion behind him, and does not take the hot
weather away with him.

But ice-men, dragon-flies and sun-flowers are happy, and never was a day so torrid that a soda-fountain
was unable to play. Yes, and scarlet geraniums!

There is one of them now, bolt-upright in an iron vase painted a comfortable color to warm you up just by looking at it, standing out in "the burden and heat of the day," and hot enough to take a helpless egg beyond the third week of incubation, and a minute or two toward the boiling-point of "eggs rare." That geranium has fairly taken fire with its scarlet flowers, and flares as happy as a torch in a triumphal procession. ·

People are never so like one another as in a heated term. They get melted down into a homogeneous mass of humanity. Had I written it "*mess*" it would have been no matter. Their angularities are fused off. They cease to be original. They say, "*Isn't* it hot!" They blow a ghost of a whistle without any *body* to it. They say, "whew!" Their collars droop like a hound's ears. They expand into broad-brimmed hats. They blossom out with umbrellas. They *festina lentè.*

The clouds come up every day, and lay their rugged heads on the rim of the horizon, and watch the landscape to see if it is done brown or done to a turn; but it isn't, and so those drowsy heads sink back, and leave the sky all clear for the setting sun to give us a parting roast at short range. How the brick walls throb and the stone pavements dance with caloric! And the earth turns over and over and fails to find a cool side. We feel the sun as it fires the east windows, and grills the roof, and sits down on every shingle, and scorches the front room, and cooks the west room, and toasts the veranda, and bakes the walls till they begin to be as much at home as they ever were in the brick-kiln.

And we are all the while watching for wind. A poplar lifts an ear of a leaf as if it heard something, and we take courage, but nothing comes of it. As a rule, the wind is always blowing somewhere else in sultry weather. If you happen to have no south window, there is just where it swings a vine or sways a tree. There is quite a breeze in the next town, and a gale in the adjoining county, possibly a tornado, but with you it is as calm as the Sea of Galilee. Fans? To be sure—but then if you have got to work them, you prefer to wait till cool weather for it. Fourth-of-July orations and fans are alike: windy but not ex-hilarating, and very fatiguing withal. Wasps, as if black rapiers should take wing, dart through the open window like shuttles through a loom. You dodge every red tongue with a dog to it, lest the attach-ment has grown mad with heat. You hunt for a cabbage-leaf for your hat lest you be sun-struck, and you grow such an absorbent of water that the leaf is about as much at home as if you were a cabbage *yourself*.

The sun has such a habit of rising that it cannot avoid it, and it comes up clear and red in the latter part of every night. If it could only spend an autumn or two in Indiana, and get "the chills," and have an intermittent fever, instead of the steady, unwinking blaze!

Peeled like an onion, to get as near as possible to the carbonate of lime without becoming an outright anatomy, I have been trying to write! My face and hands beaded with sweat like a savage's wampum; a sudorific, saline stream trickling down the pen, and diluting the ink and pickling the words, and making the wet paper as pleasant to write upon as a jelly-fish, and as appetizing to sheep as a salt-lick, I have been trying to scollop off a remembered sky with the silver edges of Colorado mountains, and give my reader a Sabbath-day's journey toward the Utah Canaan, and bid him see the great white visible throne of Pike's Peak through the red gateway of the Garden of the Gods.

Had my memories been a kid, and a mess of pottage exactly the dish to serve up on a page, it would have been brought on, piping hot from the seething kettle of the heated term. But when a man's pen can get about hot enough in the sun to brand a mule, it is time he plunged it into the trough with the blacksmith's tongs, and got the owner of the iron fingers to give him a few blasts from the bellows.

And so the glowing days burned on. The elms stood about as dusty as elephants and supple as sled-stakes. The air grew murky, and Fancy limped as if it had lost a foot. It was like holding the scythe and turning the grindstone too. Shadrach could not have lived in the third story of the house without a miracle. Meshach would not have despised the second, and Abednego would have remembered the fiery furnace had he gone to bed in the first. The building had become warmed down through. It was three layers of torrid zone.

And then I rose betimes, and, satchel in hand, climbed a huge green hill, and found welcome in a great roomy house that opened its hospitable doors to the four quarters and the thirty-two winds of heaven; and the city was under my feet, the beautiful city of Syracuse, salted and seasoned, and warranted to keep in any climate. And the winds came from the southwest and laid cool hands upon my brow, and I sat down upon a granite door-step as cold as Ponto's nose, while behold, the marble mantels in the city had been warm as a slab of new gingerbread. And the rippling grain had a cool look, and the timothy smelled sweet in the sun, and the shadow of the great house fell upon the ground like a home-made twilight, and the blessed winds came and went, and the grass gave to the feet like a king's carpet.

Then the fleecy flocks of the Lord came trooping over the unfenced edge of the western horizon, and we saw them long before the city below knew they were coming at all, and we wondered how they would wonder, and we rejoiced for them beforehand. And when the flocks were all in the home pasture over the city, the smooth wall of a blue slate-stone quarry showed along the west, and out of it, as if · there had been a door, came a troop of breezy shepherds; and the flocks were stampeded across the whole visible heaven, with the cracking of great

whips and the flicker of torches; and the roof of the
great house roared with the wind and the rain, like
a drum-corps sixty men strong, and the slanting rat-
lins of the storm were drawn taut through the air
from heaven even down to the earth, and denser than
you ever saw them in a ship's rigging; and the bowed
trees wrapped all their leaves about them as if they
had been cloaks; and the grains and grasses bent
low to keep out of the storm, and the pansies just
stood and shook with their quaint and quiet laughter,
and by-and-by the sun shone out, and lo, there is a
new heaven and a new earth!

The city that was tawny as a lion shines green
as an emerald. The smoky air is washed clean and
cool. We breathe to the bottom of our lungs, with
great respirations, as the parched yoke-bearers divert
the route of the running brook into their dry and
thirsty throats, with long drinks and great breaths
of satisfaction between. The buttons of the vest
worn a-flap and a-flare made for their holes like
prairie-dogs; the coat that had been about as intol-
erable as the shirt of Nessus was donned with a
sense of relief; and behold, I was "clothed and in
my right mind." And with a cool, dry hand, that
only yesterday was as *un*handy a member to write
with as a seal's flipper, I grasped the pen and said,
"I will write off the salted rust of the sweat from my
steel pen, as they scour a plowshare with a few
bouts in the fallow; I will record the glowing memories of the days and nights of capsicum and cay-

enne; and my gratitude for the green hill and the free winds, and the splendid rain that swept the valley of Onondaga with its royal skirts, when the rush and tumult of the storm and the bewildered and beclouded sky made it the fairest day in the calendar of a long fortnight."

What precious stuff it is they write who wish for their friends cloudless skies and gentle breezes and eternal sunshine! Who has not seen some fellow's sonnet to his girl of flesh and blood, imploring such tropical blessings upon her innocent head as could only be endured by phenixes, salamanders, and blacksmiths' anvils! Let us have sense.

CHAPTER II.

D ID you ever see a man that had been scalped?—
not by the patriarch with his scythe, but by the
savage with his knife? Well, it will not *pay* to see
him, as a general thing, unless you have a bit of blue-
closet curiosity about you, and almost everybody has.
I know a lady who goes to every funeral she can hear
of within a Sabbath-day's journey, and looks at the
deceased and watches the mourners, and determines
the depth and strength and probable length of their
sorrow. She is about as sure to be at your funeral as
she is to be at her own.

But it gives you a queer sensation, and not without a pleasant trace of horror in it, to sit beside a
well-favored gentleman, with luxuriant hair showing
around the edge of his cap, and think that a savage
once had him in his clutch with a whoop, and swept
a keen knife around his lifted locks with another
whoop, and whirled the trophy aloft with more
whoops, every atom as barbarously delighted as a
fox-hunter when he flaunts poor Reynard's "brush,"
and sounds "the treble mort." It brings back the
old border tales of the log-cabin times, you used to
hear on winter nights, when you flung an eye over

16

your shoulder as the yarn ran off, lest Black Hawk or Red Jacket, or somebody smelling of moccasins, blankets, smoke and kinnikinic, should show a red-ochre visage at a green window-pane.

That very pleasant gentleman is a conductor on the Central Pacific railroad, and beguiled the way for me as we steamed toward Ogden from the west. He ventured to a little stream two miles from a station for trout one day, and Chief-Justice Story's natural nobleman surprised him, scalped him, and left him for dead. I knew all about it, but I had a miserable desire to hear him describe the capillary calamity, though I could not quite ask him a blunt question about "the rape of the lock." I mentioned savages, if perchance he might say he knew too much of them, and then gratify my curiosity, but he had apparently forgotten the circumstance. I spoke of narrow escapes in the wilderness, but he only scratched one ear with a thoughtful finger, and pointed out a rock with a nose and chin like Voltaire's, and an eagle on a crag that looked as if he had been scalped. "Bald?" I said; "bald," he replied; and that was as near as he ever got to the subject.

It was a sunny morning when we drew up beside the depot at Ogden, where a hungry gong roared at us with a breath redolent of onion, cabbage, roast, fry and stew, and a little bell made mouths at us and gave tongue, telling of "funeral-baked meats" all cold for lunches, and we accepted the invitation.

1*

Fowls stiff and stark lay in piles, and so cerulean of breast, back and thigh, as to compel the inference that they belonged to the tribe of the Delawares, "Blue Hen's chickens" every egg of them all. The Wahsatch Mountains crowned with snow lift their thousands of feet of grandeur, and the Great Salt Lake stretches its glittering length for eighty miles, an uninhabited waste of three *ides*, three *ums* and an *ate*, to wit: chlorides of sodium, magnesium, calcium, and a sulphate of soda. But they will keep, while unhappily the fowls were kept too long. At last the locomotive whistled us aboard the Utah Central train, bound for Salt Lake City, thirty-six miles to the south. The conductor was a Mormon; also the engineer; likewise the brakeman. We looked curiously about for "signs" of the peculiar people. They were invisible. You might as well expect to catch a Baptist by baiting a trap with a water-tank as to detect the intelligent Mormon by any sanctimonious slides and cadences.

There was but one Pharisee on the train, and I am sorry to say he believed in John Calvin. A Bible in his hand, displayed to show the "Rev. X. Y. Z."; a roll of sermon protruding like a revolver from his breast-pocket: his hair parted on the "divide" of philoprogenitiveness — what a septisyllable it is! — and brought up over his ears like two little bundles of oats thrust in the elbows of a couple of barn-braces, and about ripe; the corners of his mouth curved down for pronouncing a "woe" upon somebody at sight; a wrinkle to his nose, as if a rank offense saluted him as it smelled to heaven,— there he sat, making the observer positively bilious with depravity as he watched him. Begging his pardon, I asked him the name of a place we were nearing. He made an emphatic pause before he replied, and then, with a momentous look and a deliberate air, as if he fancied he had written the Decalogue and were promulgating it for the first time, he picked his way from word to word, as if they were stepping-stones across a brook, and said, "That —place — ah — is — called — ah — Kaysville!" Fancy such a man moving you to do anything but get out of his reach, or persuading you to give anything but the cold shoulder!

A stately gentleman in black, with a pleasant look and a fatherly way — and he proved to be *exceedingly* fatherly — and with wives enough for three bishops, attracts your attention. He may be a lawyer who has clients, or a doctor who has patients, or a clergyman who can sing "A Charge to Keep I Have," but you are sure he is a prominent member of society because of the spread of his vest, as if it were buttoned over the benighted and barbarous regions of an artificial globe. He looks as if he would give you a check for a million, and you could not prevent him from doing it if you tried. He is a Mormon preacher. He came through Emigration Cañon when he was leaner. He saw this valley of abundance in the sage-brush and alkali period, before the soap-provoker had yielded to the roses of Sharon.

And the train is speeding along over the toes of the Wahsatch rugged range. The Great Salt Lake shines in the sun on the west. Evidences of fertility and abundance surround you, but it is a rugged, a sort of old Saxon abundance. There are beautiful places for beauty everywhere, but it has not risen to cultivated elegance. It is the garment with the selvedge on. Things are not square-cut and hemmed, but a little tag-locked and ragged at the edges. But there are no "lean years" in Utah. Had I visited this valley in 1847 I should have been in Mexico, but now I am in an outlying province of—Turkey.

White patches of alkaline soil show here and there; orchards dot the picture; broad pastures freckled with great herds of sleek cattle unroll. Mount Nebo lifts its tall winter one hundred and twenty miles away. Fremont's Peak is fifteen miles to the right. The Mountain of Prophecy shows its dome to the north. We are nearing the banks of the latter-day Jordan. The sharp gleam of the Lake, with its islands and its sea-gulls and its drift of clean salt, is as cooling to look at as the flash of a sword-blade. The rain here as in California is home-made. Utah goes by water.

THE TABERNACLE.

At last the gray roof of the Tabernacle shows above the trees. It is the half of a gigantic egg resting upon forty-six sandstone columns. Gentiles say it is "a *bad* egg." Build a mental bird that could lay an egg two hundred and fifty feet long and one hundred and fifty wide! It is the great egg of Utah. Between these pillars are windows and doors; open them, and nothing is left but columns and roof.

The streets of Salt Lake City are broad avenues lying square with the world, lined with beautiful trees, and bordered with streams of mountain water. Where in Christendom are the reeking gutters, in Mormondom are the clean, live brooks. But the streets were dusty, the winds were awake, and the mercury was lively. There are beautiful homes, there are adobe houses, there are many *hives*.

It was Sunday, and we went to the Tabernacle. The great oval structure, sixty-five feet to the roof, was dressed in the gloomy pomp of mourning for the dead president, Brigham Young. Immense funeral wreaths depended from the ceiling. The great dais, raised tier above tier, was draped in black, and upon it were seated the Twelve, and the Elders and Bishops of the Church of Mormon. And they were an impressive and dignified body of men. John Taylor with his frosty crown; Orson Pratt looking over the gray hedge of a mighty beard; John Sharp, shrewd, angular and genial; George Q. Cannon, clean-looking, amiable, and winning in his ways. He had a word to say about tithes, and rallied up the stone-masons to work upon the new Temple. But you would suppose from the pleasant way he talked that he was not calling for ten per cent of back-ache, tug and trowel; but explaining how every man could be his own doctor or lawyer, or could get more money for eight hours' work than he could possibly earn in ten. Take the great Sanhedrim together, it looked legislative enough to be a Senate. The black background was dotted with white heads. There was now and then a bullet-head or a chuckle-head, but of the majority, some of them might have been Baptist deacons, or Methodist ministers, or Presbyterian dominies, or presidents of colleges. Behind them towered the great organ in its trappings of woe. Built where it stands, it rises like a castle, one of the great musical instruments of the world. The fine choir of adults clustered about its base looked like boys and girls, and when the mellow thunder of the deep bass rolled out, and all the birds and flutes locked up in it were let loose above the surf of sound, and the warble of the human voices came out in the lulls, it was very grand.

But the master-spirit of the dais had abdicated. Brigham Young was not there. Coarse and strong, with wonderful executive powers, of an earnest and dogged purpose that never let go, a self-reliance that breasted storm and bearded wilderness, nothing if not resolute, knowing what men were fitted to his use, and building them in the wall of his design as a mason lays the stone, he brought the most heteroge-neous elements into harmony, taught a Babel of tongues to talk Mormon with one accord, left a bloom-ing garden where he found a wilderness that grew ghastly pale at its own desolation, founded the mid-continental city of America, and hastened the building of the iron highway from Atlantic to Pacific a whole generation of men.

THE PEOPLE.

I hoped John Taylor would preach, but a nephew of Smith of the tribe of Joseph, who had been on a mission to Europe, cumbered the ground. A pale, lank-sided fanatic, who railed at the Gentiles with venomous bitterness as only a bloodless man *can* rail, and the fiercer he talked the paler he grew, till his waxen face, relieved upon the black drapery, gave the grotesque effect of a medallion-head escaping from the medal, becoming animate and angry, and bobbing about upon the jet velvet like the rolling eyeballs of Othello.

But if Smith was not worth hearing, the great audience was a memorable sight. Fancy six thousand faces fitted into an ellipse that will seat eight thousand people,—a huge mosaic of human heads! There were at least a thousand children among them, sorted off with picket-lines of mothers between, and about four-score infants in arms. It would have been an appetizing sight for Herod, and would have kept the baby-eating Saturn in rations for three months. Every style of dress was represented, from the old poke-bonnet with a puckered face in its back room to the wafer of a hat with a butterfly on it, and the lamp-mat trifle just caught on the bump of approbativeness behind. There was the old beaver chafed bare in spots, as if it had worked in harness some time, and the new silk that shines like a bottle. There was the modern girl hung about with two or three dresses of different lengths and divers colors, and curiously caught up with half-reefs here and there, as if a sailor had been taking in the top-hamper for a storm and got blown overboard in the act. There was the strait, scant skirt of the ancient girl collapsed about her form like a balloon with the valve gone. Aggregate a hundred school-house and four-corners country audiences of thirty years ago, sprinkle in a few city people here and there, and you have an idea of that great congregation.

You will look in vain for facial signs of utter misery. There are sad-eyed, weary-looking women, and so there are everywhere. You can pick out many a devout believer who came through the wilderness of old. You can detect the honest doubters and the foxy professors and the sincere worshipers. Drawn largely from the laboring classes of Europe, any considerable intelligence and culture cannot be found in the rank and file, but it is an error to think this has not remarkable exceptions. There are astronomers and naturalists of no mean order; linguists that could grace a professor's chair in eastern universities; men of general cultivation and large business ability, and women of refinement.

But the children are a marvelous product. You ride along the beautiful avenues and see groups of them, neatly dressed and bright as quicksilver, playing in the shade. You meet clusters of Brigham

Young's grandchildren; you encounter his sons and daughters. Every girl is half-sister to somebody, and a boy's father may be his uncle, and his mother own aunt to his half-brother. The ward schools swarm with children. A large and efficient Episcopal school numbers its pupils by hundreds, many of whose parents are Mormons, for about five-sixths of the people are "Saints." Take a flock of sheep in the pleasant April days, flecked white with lambs, each saying its *a-b-abs* for its mother, and you have the picture.

The communion service is celebrated every Sunday, and while Smith was yet preaching, the cup-bearers with silver pitchers of water were noiselessly serving the multitude, of which every one partook, even to the infant in arms. Then the last hymn was sung, the benediction said, and the great congregation poured out from every side like ants from a disturbed hill, and the Tabernacle was solemn and empty as a cave.

The death of Brigham Young was confidently believed to mark the beginning of the end of Mormonism; that individual ambitions and jealousies would explode the system like a bomb. But it is not true. When the delusion is dispelled it will not be by earthquake shock or government enactment or meditating bayonets, but because the incoming Gentile tide will wash out of it all its color and its strength, and the Gentile sun will draw it up in a misty cloud, and the free winds of the world will blow it quite away.

2

THE UTAH INDIAN.

The tribes of Utah were Brigham Young's fast friends. Whatever he did, he never broke a promise to them, and they became his faithful allies. The night after his death the Indians kindled signal fires along the mountain peaks, and thus telegraphed the event eighty miles down the valley. An old chief who had known Young since he entered the wilderness came up by the train the next day, and, accosting no one, went directly to the president's mansion. John W. Young met him at the door. "Want to see Brigham." "Father is dead," said the son. "Let me see him," persisted the chief. "Well, come in," and the Indian straightened his blanket, smoothed back his hair, drew himself up, and said, "Ready."

Entering the room, he took in everything without turning an eye, and asked: "Where Brigham?" "In this box," was the answer. He approached, laid his hand upon it, and said: "Brigham dead? He here?" and then, when his doubt was dispelled, he shook with emotion as no paleface ever saw a savage moved before, his broad chest heaved, and with the exclamation, "Brigham dead! Brigham dead!" he burst into tears, fairly convulsed with grief. The son stood silently by until the chief, measurably controlling his emotion, readjusted his blanket, gave one look at the casket, and saying, "Me go home,—tell people Brigham dead. Be much cry there," left the house, went direct to the depot where the southward-bound train was just whistling to go, stepped aboard and was gone with the tidings.

The Indians on the railroads of the far West ride free. They are D. H's, to wit, dead-heads. The scale is graduated thus: hedgers, ditchers and writers, full fare; clergymen, half fare; Indians, editors and infants, scot-free. The managers of the roads act wisely in issuing "complimentaries" to the Indians. Incessantly roaming about, they become invaluable police at large. If anything is wrong with rail, bridge or culvert, or any obstructions are placed upon the track, their runners are sure to warn the engineer and prevent the catastrophe. Every paleface who rides upon the trains may be glad that the savages and the editors are friends to the railroad. Not a few narrow escapes have become matters of public news by this route: an Indian told the engineer, the engineer told the conductor, the conductor told the editor, and the printer told the world.

The desert of thirty years ago, walled in by mountains, inaccessible by distance, is a city to-day of twenty thousand. The locomotive has found it, the trained lightning has struck it, fashion has overtaken it, the Gentiles are at its doors. Its broad avenues, with their twin brooklets and their double lines of shade trees, are traversed by street cars, its dwellings are nested in gardens, shrubbery and flowers, its people extend the open hand of welcome. You hear the prayers of our fathers and the songs of our mothers, and there is little outdoor evidence that you are in a

city whose religion is as oriental and corrupt as the
faith of the Moslem.

I do not know whether it has been remarked that
the children of a polygamous alliance more frequently
resemble their mothers, but I think observation will
establish the fact. The Sabbath is quite as rigidly
observed in Salt Lake City as in any average village
in New York, and far better than in Chicago or the
majority of large cities in the East, and little presents
itself to offend the most fastidious. Scenes of de-
bauchery are unknown. In the ordinary sense of the
word, the women of the old Mormon stock are fiercely
virtuous. Since the advent of Gentiles and miners,
in several regards the slippers are worn a little easier
and a trifle more down at the heel. Altogether, the
city is remarkably well governed.

A lively and ludicrous warfare is kept up between
the Gentiles and the Mormons. What the former lack
in numbers they make up in bantam-like *vim*. Mer-
chandise is brought down almost to the zero of eastern
prices, and a traveler direct from California, where he
is expected to *buy* a section of the hotel in which he
sojourns, is astonished at the Utah moderation of
twenty shillings a day. If there is danger of a lull
in the battle, the papers all around the board trumpet
the forces to a new charge, and they are sharp, saucy
and aggressive as hornets in a heated term.

CAMP DOUGLAS.

We crossed the city with the river Jordan at its feet, and the mountains standing off from it in a stately way on the east, and climbing seven hundred feet, and two miles out, we bowled in upon the splendid parade ground of Camp Douglas. As neat as a nobleman's lawn it is, with its well-appointed barracks, its commodious and elegant officers' quarters, the tidy uniforms of the boys in blue, the old-time clank of swords, and over all, glowing in the setting sun, the most beautiful flag in the universe, always saving and excepting the white banner of the Prince of Peace. To tell the truth, I had not felt as if I were in the United States since entering Utah, till I struck the camp and saw the flag and heard the concordant regimental band, as it gave "The Red, White and Blue" to the mountains that played it back, and the city that listened for it, and the setting sun that marched to it down the western slope.

And then the great kennels of cannon — not a Quaker among them — long-range fellows with their noses toward the city waiting for orders. They gave me a comfortable feeling when I stood at the right end of them, for me, which is the wrong end for business. The city lies at my feet like a great white flock tangled in the shrubbery; the sheen of the lake; the twinkle of the river; the air glorified as if an evening cloud had stained it fast colors; the gateless Gaza of Emigration Cañon yawning below the camp,

through which the travel-worn vanguard rode thirty
years ago, and came out from the ruggedness and
shadow of ravines into the sunshine and calm of that
Mormon misnomer, the Promised Land. Altogether
it is a beautiful picture, and not easy to be forgotten.
And then we rattled down into the valley and back
to the hotel in the cool of the night, and the next
morning were away for Ogden, and well out of Mormondom, with its border struggles, its dark and bloody
ground, the unuttered sorrows of women and the
gloom of homes that are loveless. That it can exist
and not contaminate the body politic is one of the
strangest imaginable gauges in a christian land to
measure the greatness of the Republic.

CHAPTER III.

DENVER.

IT was at Cheyenne that we got our first steak of the black-tailed deer—rich, juicy, dark, a luxury; and yet I am frank enough to confess that a bit of Southdown mutton, or even one ewe lamb garnished with June peas, suits me quite as well. There was antelope also,—that timid little lady of the genus *cervus;* but I think Thackeray, after seeing the graceful creatures shaking their glimpse of white handkerchief at him, turning to watch him with a touch of human and feminine curiosity, and then bounding over the plains as light as thistle-downs, might have said he would about as soon dine off of a fine young woman.

We take the train for Denver, one hundred and six miles south, and nearly a thousand feet down from Cheyenne, and are careering over the rolling plains and getting down-stairs by the run. We are in Colorado, the Centennial and the Silver State. We pass a town as much the child of "H. G." as the New York *Tribune*. It is Greeley, with its hundred thousand acres of fertile land checkered off with trees and traversed by trenches of water. Some years, it has

31

kept a grasshopper boarding-house, and occasionally there has been "a nipping and an eager air," but its general prosperity has been signal. Its harvests go by water, and so do the *people*. Greeley, therefore, is loafer-proof.

A few more swift dives and we reach Denver, and almost a mile above the level of the sea. It is the marvel of mountain cities. Nineteen years ago its site was an utter wilderness. To-day it is a young metropolis, the capital of a state bound to be opulent and great, a population that crowds twenty-five thousand, a vigorous press, and a great deal of it,—I can remember when a copy of the *Rocky Mountain News* seemed to belong to a menagerie of grizzly bears and mountain lions, as much a desert production as "the pelican of the wilderness,"—the hub of a railroad system that *spokes* the state; churches, schools, street railways, business, nerve, culture, refinement and a future. Set down in it at night, the gaslight dazzles you, the hotel cries assail you, the city astonishes you. It is an eastern city to which mountain shoulders have given a big lift. The air is as pure as the wine at the wedding in Cana. It has tonic and tingle. It is like Cowper's tea: it "cheers but not inebriates," and if there ever was an awkward, toggle-jointed sentence, it is that analysis of the poet's "cup." The American Hotel took us in, and we were comfortable at a shake of the bell—"rest and a shelter, food and fire." Let us take pattern from Bunyan's fellow with the muck-rake just at first, and not look up, for there are angels in the air, and we may not care to look down.

A PRAIRIE-DOG ECHO.

There are coughs and coughs. There are the cough of derision, the cough of doubt, and the cough of embarrassment; the cough that helps a halting speaker to bridge the little cañon between one sentence he is puzzled to end and another he doesn't know how to begin, where his thought has tumbled through into the gulf of bewilderment; the racking cough that goes before the coffin as the drum-major before the corps. Let not the compositor lay out the band by spelling that corps with an *e*. There is yet another cough, which may be called the cough colloquial and Coloradan. It is more frequent in conversation than profanity in the society of canal-horses. In your hotel at Denver you hear people coughing along the halls, — coughs masculine, feminine and neuter; a hollow cough in a distant room, a hacking cough in the office, a smothered cough in the cellar, a subdued cough in the garret, a guttural cough which is Hebrew, a cough in the roof of the mouth which is like the last note of "the cock's shrill clarion" in Gray's Elegy. You meet people of deliberate step and feeble breath; people whose respiration rustles like a silk dress, or pants like the ghost of a steam-boat. You enter the well-filled stores, and are served by men who punctuate their pleasant courtesy with small commas of cough, or bits of ahems, or interjections of sneeze. Denver seems to be an outlying province of Swift's Houyhnhnms — pronounced *hooinmz*, with a whinnying quaver on the *n*—and you begin to get nervous and ask questions. But when you learn that all these coughers and wheezers and sneezers came up hither for health not long ago, with hardly strength enough to bark above their breath, and that they are improving with might and main, you are comforted and composed. I meet eastern friends who are perfectly well, but came here in wretched plight. "But why don't you go home?" "Ah, that's the rub! We have *kept* going home,—slipped back every time, like the frog in the well, into the old trouble, and returned to brace up." I encounter several officers of the same name, and all Generals — there are two in sight this minute — who can live nowhere else; a name as common as John Smith, for it is General Debility. It is astonishing how feverish a man grows to escape from a capital place when he finds it impossible; but between death and Colorado, the last is everybody's first choice.

JEWELRY.

Lapidaries abound. At almost every corner you see rich displays of Colorado "specimens," from tiger-cats to moss-agates. Rings, pins, charms, chains, set with smoky topazes, agates, onyxes—which are nothing like lynxes—garnets, opals, amethysts, jaspers, and bits of petrified woods. You see crystals of topaz that weigh ten pounds, and gulch and mountain are full of gem-hunters who, armed with hammer and knapsack, take twenty-mile tramps for the treasures. And there is curious excitement in it like watching a game of chance. You pick up a rusty gray stone, knock off the clinging sand, and pocket it with a doubt. The lapidary may tell you it is a choice moss-agate, or a pebble just right to shie at a sparrow. The mountain jewelry trade engages many hands, and much skill and taste. A tourist abroad has a royal way, you know, of buying things for ten dollars that, returning home, he finds he could purchase around the corner for eight. And so it comes to pass there are "millions in it."

When that hobble-de-hoy of yours was a baby, Colorado was a wilderness that howled, and I have been attending the State Fair of that same Colorado. The law of limitation has apparently been suspended; the cabbages are larger than many of Dr. Peters' asteroids — to the naked eye; three ears of the clean white corn would make a club for Hercules; the wheat is fit to be asked for in the universal petition; the products of the dairy are admirable, and I was prepared to expect it, for if ever a State exemplified the proverb, "there is room at the top," it is Colorado. I was in her sky pastures a mile and a half above the sea, where thousands of cattle round up like the moon at the full. But the geological department was simply magnificent. The precious metals lay about in boulder, nugget, crystal and powder. Almost every description of gem but the diamond mocked the rainbow, and lay about amid all beautiful shapes and crystals of quartz, lead, iron and coal. About every letter of the alphabet that spells e-a-r-t-h was represented.

And the people were there by thousands, and then more thousands. They are an English-speaking people, they are *our* people, cordial, hospitable, with the first love not died out of them. What we love at a thousand miles away we forget at three thousand. Seven days and nights are a little too long a range for Cupid's common arrows unless he puts more strength in the bow.

CHAPTER IV.

YOU shall be riding in a street-car through the city of Denver on a double-eagle of a day, clean gold and fresh from the Mint. The trees have shaken out all sail for the summer. The bees are booming about among the flowers. The children are playing in the shade. The grind of the wheels of commerce— and the street-car—is in your ears, and you look through the window into the invisible air, not one midge or mote to a sunbeam. You shall see an arc of the western horizon jagged, scolloped and broken down with mountains all dusted and drifted with everlasting snows. You shall see the white billows of innumerable winters, as they seem tumbling on in stupendous silence to whelm the world. If there could be such a thing, and anybody could comprehend it, I should say it is *a picture of thunder.* And yet there is no suggestion of tumult, as the words imply, but rather of a comforting stability and an unspeakable calm. Like death they have "all seasons for their own," and stand and triumph over a turbulent world. What surges must have broken over the prow of this planet at some time, till the Arctic caught them in the act and struck them with frost, and there

37

they hang about the bows of the craft through the ages, the pale corpses of the troubled and disastered sea. And behold, the Arctic is here beneath the all-day sun!

LONG'S PEAK.

Had the founders of Denver meant nothing more than to sit down and have a lifelong look at the grandest mountains on the continent, they could not have chosen better. Here is an amphitheatre with a sweep of three hundred miles of peaks and crowns and towers and crags, not one of them withdrawn beyond the range of an immediate presence. In this perfect air human vision is as keen as an eagle's. The eye " carries" two days' journey and does instant execution. You sit in the car, and looking northwest behold the white-helmeted poll of Long's Peak fending off the sky with a lift of two and two-thirds miles above the sea. It is eighty miles away, but as palpable and distinct as a picture on your parlor wall. You see the shadows lying under the lee of the mountain. You see the black gashes of old battles with earthquake and lightning; you note where the glaring white tones down into sandstone red and granite gray. You see the maroons and the blue velvets, and all the trickery and enchantment of light, distance and shadow. You discern the timber line, where vegetation dwarfs itself in a fight for life and a foothold, as if huge grenadiers should dwindle down to drummer-boys in the front. You can make out the

columns of tall timber farther down. You can watch
the clouds around the mountain shoulders like one of
the smothering ruffs of Queen Elizabeth. And it is
eighty miles away!

And we talk of its vastness, while, if piled peak
upon peak, it would take ninety thousand Longs to
reach the moon, whose lakes men have meandered
without going from home. Ah, there is plenty of
room in the sky-parlors, and Denver is a splendid
place to study anatomy and count the spinous pro-
cesses in the continent's backbone.

PIKE'S PEAK.

Then, turning to the southwest, Pike's Peak, the
mighty milestone and monument to thousands of the
old miners, stands erect and flat-footed upon the world.
It is seventy-five miles to his base, but the view is
as clean-cut and clear as a cameo. Should I tell
anybody it is 13,985 feet high, it would be no very
satisfying information: should I say, You must climb
about twelve miles to reach the summit, it would be
better; but suppose the reader swings a little tea-
kettle over a fire on the sea-beach, metonymically,
it will boil at 212°. Now pick up kettle, kindling-
wood and thermometer, and begin your climb. At
5,300 feet the water is in active trouble at 202°.
Playing Longfellow's young man, Excelsior, again, at
the altitude of 10,600 feet it is in a lively state of
unrest at 192°. Another lift to the top of the Peak,
and the peripatetic kettle makes a tambourine of the

lid and plays so mild a tune that what scalded you promptly and satisfactorily down by the sea will be no hotter than the tea strong enough to "bear up an egg," wherewith our grandmothers chinked up their hearts and limbered their tongues after a big washing.

How often lofty people forget that ebullition does not always mean earnestness and fervor. Boiling water is not necessarily hot water.

Pike's Peak is not the tallest of the white Carmelites of the mountains, but he is the omnipresent peak of Colorado. He follows you wherever you go. You catch a glimpse of him from the north at a distance of a hundred miles. Fine as a piece of choice old china, it is a page of solid geometry torn from the book and magnified and glorified; a true cone of pure silver. He confronts you on the west. He is sixty miles nearer, but seems no grander than before. He is an unscalable peak still. He seems to be standing off and on, and waiting for you at all points. But when you draw near, Pike loses his symmetry and shows rugged and irregular. What seemed a stately white tent for the occupancy of angels camping out for a picnic is turned into a mighty cairn of crags and boulders. The peak is blunted to a great stone-yard of eighty acres, and as poor plowing as a pyramid. But it is a trick of all mountains to strike their peaks as you approach. It is only when you leave them in the distance that their swelling grandeur returns.

Tall mountains and great men are alike. They show best a great way off. Never climb a mountain to see its peak. You may as well hope to kindle a fire with chips from the North Pole.

" COLORADO SPRINGS."

Taking the Denver and Rio Grande railroad, a cunning narrow-gauge, while its officers are broad-gauge, you pass the Rocky Range in review, count peaks thick as stacks of grain in a rich harvest; look across the upper edge and dry side of rain storms to the ridges beyond; run down the line seventy-six miles to a place called Colorado Springs, because it *has* none, and to Colorado City, because it *is* none. The former is a beautiful prairie town; the latter, the old Territorial capital, is shrunken and rusty, the paint worn off and the pluck worn out. Nothing but a politician out of business is more forlorn than a deserted capital.

A stage is waiting for you at the dry Springs, like a lighter around a ship, to take you six miles to Manitou. You step upon the platform, and there stands Pike waiting for you. He is only eighteen miles off, and so you step on his toes when you touch the ground. Colorado Springs might be a fine prairie village in Illinois, if it did not happen to be in Colorado. It has a frontispiece of " specimens " and " views " to tempt the tourist. Heaps of geology abound, at prices so long that you need " a pocket full of rocks " to *begin* with. And then you go up hill. There is a feeling of snow in the air, but the fields are in bloom. You look away to the Peak, and see a snowstorm drawn in chalk lines between you

2*

and the mountain. It is a profile, a genuine cartoon, of a piece of winter weather. But that snow never touches ground. It weeps itself away in a slow drizzle. It is a white shawl dripping with fringes of water.

Manitou, where the springs really are, is an exquisite nestling-place in the mountains. Of course, Pike is standing before the door of your hotel. The great rock-bowl of splendid soda, grand enough to grace a symposium of the whole Pantheon, is a minute's walk distant. Its edges are chased with silver-white soda, for it always sparkles and forever overflows. Up a beautiful glen are the great iron springs whose waters will turn a clear glass goblet into an amber-tinted beauty, and as fast colors as an Ethiop's skin. I think a man might swallow water enough in three months to make a respectable lightning-rod of himself, and cheat those modest peripatetics with thunder-gust bayonets out of a bargain. It is said there is sufficient iron in a man's blood, anyhow, to make a shot to kill him, and why shouldn't that water make hardware of him altogether? There are spacious hotels, cozy cottages, delightful lounging-places, shaded paths and beautiful views at Manitou. It is worth two Saratogas for health and recreation.

THE MOUNTAIN HOME.

Living twelve miles up the world from this retreat were two valued friends of "lang syne," and the desire to see them was stronger than gravitation, so up we went through the Ute Pass to find them. The Pass is a narrow cañon overhung with rocks, overarched

with trees, now roofed with not more than twenty
feet of blue sky, now turning under hoods of crags,
now out into little bays full of tangled luxuriance.
Aspens all along shake in their shoes, and pines give
their same old sigh. The splendid road has more
crooks than the horn that jarred down Jericho's walls,
and it goes through throats of places that make you
feel for your windpipe. We met two things when
climbing the Pass. One was a storm that threw one
solitary thunder down the gorge from top to bottom
without striking a stair. It was startling as if a rifle-
cannon should call you to breakfast. The other was
an eccentric, sparkling stream that leaped and flashed
from ledge to ledge at our left. Here, it came fifty
feet at a tumble; there, it splintered like a lance
against a crag; yonder, it darted bright as silver;
now, it lurked black as ink; then, it was fleecy as
Jason's sheep; again, it was smooth as a looking-
glass. It confronted you, it flanked you, it was an
incessant surprise, and a success also.

So we climbed through, and out into the rolling
country, but always up, meeting greasy Mexicans with
long double-files of lean mules and leaner oxen drawing ore down to the railroad; meeting solitary horse-
men; seeing cabins and pleasant homes here and
there, until we were nine thousand feet above the sea,
and that Pike was waiting for us at the end of our
journey! We saw the scar of a trail, and a dished
landscape, like a foot-bath at the feet of the Peak,
and a long, low, broad-brimmed house with a home-

like look and neat out-buildings about it, and a white
tent like a big mushroom. It was our friend's eyrie,
and we were made welcome.

Soon night came up, for in the mountains it never
comes *down*. Had Homer—who was *Homer?*—been
a Coloradan, he would never have said the god "came
down like night." First, the valley below filled with
darkness; then, the basin we were served up in; then,
the dish overflowed, and the tide of shadow slowly
rose along the mountain sides. We were over head
and ears, fairly drowned in night, but Pike's snow-
cap yet glittered in the sun. The unclouded sky
had not blossomed out with celestial asters. By-and-
by the mountain was up to his shoulders in darkness, and then he doffed his white cap for a turban
of red kerchief that slowly faded to a dim, cold gray,
and it was night all over. Then the voices of noc-
turnal birds startled the stillness, the long whine of
a mountain lion up the cañon, the bay of a dog down
the valley, and a score of indescribable rustlings and
whisperings, made the silence lonely and audible.

We had climbed out of the world of railroad and
telegraph. We had gotten into the back chamber of
the century. And—oh, the delight of it!—we had
escaped the hammer and the clangor, the banging
and the twanging of the wires ever clanging, the
wires ever wrangling. That forty-fingered girl with
her piano had not found us out. There was nothing above us but the signal station and the stars.
It was a new sensation.

Entering the house we sat down like four signs of the zodiac around the generous fireplace, and torches of light pine flung their clear white splendors everywhere, till the house shone like an engine's headlight. Talk of the golden illumination of wax candles, and the glare of gas chandeliers! There is nothing so brilliantly beautiful as the fat pine fire by night. It is more than heat and light. It is cheerfulness, comfort, company and content. The remembrance of that fireside shines like an evening star in the mountains. May those that kindled it ever have an abiding star for all the nights of their two lives, that "goes not down nor hides obscured among the tempest of the sky, but melts away into the light of heaven." That far-off scene is as near as the left breast. The two trout-ponds, gorgeous with fish that must have been caught out in the crimson and golden rain of Danaë and been speckled for life; the prairie-dog village up the road;—they were "not at home," the four-footed prevaricators!—the great furnaces of lime and charcoal, the ebony and alabaster of the mountains; the clear sweet air, that you want a great deal of if you run a race; the complete escape from the elbows and turbulence of the world; the boyish expectancy, on tip-toe for something to prowl down the cañon, or lumber out of the woods, or steal forth from the cleft rocks, say a cinnamon bear or a mountain lion; the stateliness of Pike; the friends we found there;—all make an enduring picture and a delicious memory.

CHAPTER V.

AN hour's drive from Manitou brought us into an up-hill and down-dale region full of rocks in all grotesque shapes and tints; red, gray, pink, yellow, dead white; the eloquent evidences of disturbances in days so long ago that almanacs do not name them, when something put a shoulder to the strata of rocks and lifted them out to the light; and here they are, gnawed by the elements, carved in fantastic forms innumerable. The lower stratum of sandstone was more edible than the upper that rests upon it, and so winds, rains, frosts and suns have eaten it out, and left necks upon which are mounted masses of the more durable rock, curved, rounded, poised and perched upon the lean, long, uncanny necks.

Think of a multitude of stone toadstools, six, ten, twelve feet in diameter; of Chinamen's hats done in pink, yellow, red, with mossy rosettes; of awkward sun-bonnets weighing two tons apiece, always slipping off and never falling; of stone bowls, big as caldron kettles, bottom side up on pillars; of ogreish heads wrapped about with gray turbans; of loaves of over-done bread, two hundred pounds apiece, set upon the rocks to cool; of a crop of capped and hooded gate-

posts waiting to be harvested; of petrified dumb-bells
such as Jupiter might have practiced with before
throwing his thunderbolts; of a flock of witches in
red tatters squatting around in dumb petrefaction;
of masses of rock as big as a house poised upon stones
the size of a pumpkin; of whole families of Leaning
Towers — no end of Pisas — *accenting* everything in a
manner more emphatic than delightful; — think of all
these at once, and you will know something of this
sandstone nightmare.

In and out we go among these queer leavings and
carvings of what were once solid books of stone. Did
you ever see an old volume that the book-worm had
tunneled and honeycombed? Do you remember how
spangly the maple-sugar was when ladled out upon
snow or dropped into water? It is a jumble of ideas,
and so are these sandstone jokes, jests, frolics and
fritters. Here is Mrs. Grundy's head, her chisel of a
chin and her incisive nose threatening each other
across a long unhemmed mouth; and tongue, head,
cap and all, dumb and motionless in a blessed sandstone silence. Alas, that it is not the ubiquitous lady
indeed, that no more the question should be heard,
"What will Mrs. Grundy say?" There is Napoleon's
hat. It weighs five hundred pounds if it weighs an
ounce. There is a prehistoric look about things, and
you feel as if you are four hundred years old yourself.
You are afraid some of those Saracen heads will cry
"Bismillah!"—the baker come out to look after his
loaves—the toads leap forth and sit upon their

stools — Mrs. Grundy prove not to be so very dead, or you turn into old red sandstone for other tourists to look at and laugh about.

We are nearing the gate of the "Garden of the Gods. Some people have a masterly faculty for mis-naming things. Whether it is a baby or a bowlder to be christened, the names they bestow could be interchanged without exciting a suspicion that either had been wronged. "Garden of the Gods" is about as appropriate as Orchard of Hesperus or the Valley of Rasselas. It suggests nothing, and it means all it suggests. Here is a park of five hundred acres of land, mountain-locked on the north and west, moated with cañons on the south, and walled with red sand-stone on the east, spread with grassy carpets here and there, and dotted with little pines and other vegetable stragglers. You approach a gateway two hundred feet wide, with red sandstone towers three hundred feet high, covered with sculptures that no man can read, and massive and rugged as are no other portals in the world.

In the center of the way is a red pillar twenty-five feet high, which was probably the horse-block whence the Titanesses stepped to the pillions behind their lords and masters when they went their morning rides. You can see the walled-up windows whence the old warders looked forth. You can see escutch-eons that no herald can make out; chimneys standing alone; towers dismantled; alcoves, broken arches, pinnacles, castle ruins, and all red as porphyry. And a little way off you see parallel walls that are marble white, and show in fine contrast with the cinnabar tints around.

Not long ago I saw photographs of the ruins of Ba'albek, and I said, a greater than Ba'albek is here; these Titanic castles and fortresses wrecked and ruined, and greater in their destruction than the completed architecture of the Wrens and Walters of modern times. Anybody can rear castles from foundation to turret, but only one architect can build ruins so grand, and his name is Upheaval.

It was a splendid morning when we stood in front of the gateless Gaza, with its green lawn. A couple of men of standard stature walked through, and turned dwarfs as they went. At the right was a monumental group such as Cruikshank might have designed as the Graveyard of the Grotesque. But we halted in front of the grand entrance. There, set in a red frame, though eighteen miles away, was a royal presence. A vast white pavilion rose against the blue sky, as if the Titans had gone into grand encampment. Never was a fairer picture mounted in a more befitting frame. All galleries of art fade into insignificance. All works of the old scenic masters are trifles as you gaze upon this. It was so restful and complete. It filled the eye and the soul as well. But it was not like Longfellow's pavilion when he sang:

3

"But when the old cathedral bell
    Proclaimed the morning prayer,
The white pavilion rose and fell
    On the alarmed air."

This tent was motionless as the arch of heaven, for it was PIKE'S PEAK in a frame of porphyry!

Let us take the noble legend of the State of Colorado and engrave it beneath the picture: *Nil sine Numine.*

My recollections of Colorado are of the pleasantest. I am glad I have lived to see her born into the Union, and as I took occasion to write a year or two ago, in alluding to the Centennial Exposition:

Egypt! Earth's own eldest daughter,
    Colorado, silver bride!
One mountain-born and one of water,
    Eldest — youngest — side by side.
By one star more Centennial given,
    Colorado's Silver State
Has reïnforced the mimic heaven,
    And the Flag strikes THIRTY-EIGHT!

CHAPTER VI.

HATS.

THE manner in which certain excellent people lifted their hats forty years ago is of little moment; of *too* little, you must think, to need a pair of adjectives, reverently and carefully, to describe it, but why "carefully"? They were not silk hats, but either felt or genuine beaver that had made jackets for the four-footed dam-builders and millwrights; beaver that would last four-and-twenty years without shedding their fur.

Take the roomy bell-crowns, that flared like an old-time wooden churn bottom side up. They were *safes* and *postoffices*. In the garrets of those hats were deposited the letters received in a whole quarter, the huge fellows about as long and broad as a brick. There notes of hand, memoranda, accounts, were filed away. The men, most of them, stood sturdily on their legs in those days, and so were not top-heavy in the least. A red bandana sparsely dotted with white spots was also carried in the hat. When the castor was in position, there were three strata of commodities: first, letters and papers; second, textile fabrics; last and lowest, the head. There were two ways of unroofing a man without emptying the garret; either he removed the hat, giving at the instant a little duck of the head, or he put up a hand as he careened the beaver, ready to catch whatever might tumble. The latter looked a little awkward, since it gave him the appearance of wanting to catch something alive, that might lurk in the loft.

Nothing you wear comes to resemble you so nearly as the hat; not the "soft" variety; that is as stupid and devoid of character as a meal-bag; but the firmer fabric that "sets itself aright," and is gradually fashioned to your phrenology, flaring out at your caution, curving away in front of your perceptives, or rounding out behind your love of children and — grown people.

You have worn for a minute one of those brass hats, about as cumbrous as a king's crown, that, as the hatter adjusts it upon your head, dots a profile, a sort of ground plan of the cerebral regions, upon a piece of paper in the top of it. Did you much admire that line-fence of your faculties thus portrayed? Sometimes it is shaped like the print of a moccasin with an awkward foot in it, and sometimes like the anatomy of a sap-trough. A double Yankee inheritance would never enable you to guess what it was meant to picture, whether a kidney-bean or the track of a plantigrade, but a human head never!

Hats, like their wearers, have grown ephemeral. Once they lived as long as good dogs live, but now their average age is about six months. I respect a hat that has seen service, that has been worn evenly

and steadily winter and summer, that has a whitish
suspicion of edges, and has so accommodated itself
to the wearer and grown nobby with his faculties,
that he quite forgets he is not bareheaded. Find
that hat drifting about on the mill-pond, and you
immediately know whose body you are going to drag
for. There is no more poetry in a hat of the firm
variety than there is in a half-joint of stove-pipe.
You cannot fancy the hero of a hundred battles in
a silk hat. The very name of the article has a dis-
reputable rhyming acquaintance with such words as
bat, cat, flat, gnat, rat, scat and sprat. "Stick a
feather in it," and it is hat still. Wreathe it like
Billy Barlow's:

"All round my hat I wears a weeping willow,"

but it will not do.

> "He put his hat upon his head,
> And walked into the Strand,
> And there he met another man
> Whose hat was in his hand."

Two hats in the same stanza, and two men with
immortal souls engaged in carrying those hats in two
different ways, is too much. But make them helmets
and call them Greeks, or plumed bonnets and call
them Scots, or shadow-shedding sombreros and name
them bandits, and there is an element of romance
and poetry that may possibly float the article on the
rhythmic current. The tall hats of the Puritans have
no more grace than a funnel, and the leafless pictures

of the Pilgrim Fathers freezing about Plymouth Rock
and towering up in their peaked hats always reminded
me of something rank run up to seed in the fall.

Figuring in political history, the hat has been
garnished with the black cockade and the buck-tail.
The crape "weeper" used to swing from it, and, as
the mourner walked, sway in a slow and pensive way
from side to side, like a black rudder without a
helmsman. It is reverently lifted to sorrow, beauty
and death. It is whirled about the head in visible
huzzas, and shied enthusiastically into the air like a
rocket. It is held forth for alms, and, muffled with
a handkerchief lest you should hear the jingle of
ignoble pennies, is passed about in the beneficent
congregation. The mettled racers used to burst from
the grand stand at the "drop of the hat."

One family in the British Empire has the privi-
lege of appearing covered in the presence of royalty,
and all the old Quakers wore the broad-brim unrebuked in the presence of God and man.

When the wearer cocks his hat over his right eyebrow it means defiance, if it doesn't mean — a fool.
If he sets it squarely upon his head and pulls it
down like a percussion cap to the tips of his ears, it
is determination, if it is not—doggedness. Let down
the hammer upon that hat, and he will explode. If
he throws it back upon the nape of his neck like
the calash-top of a chaise, it signifies a careless inde-
pendence and a propensity to "face the music" with
his whole countenance.

CHAPTER VII.

THERE is a fatal facility about grooves. They arc wonderfully easy things to run in. They are labor-savers and man-savers. They save time, trouble, bravery and brains. It is as if rivers ran down stream both ways, and oars had never been invented.

The groove-bound doctor attacks the patient in typhoid fever according to a formula so old as to be mossy, and the result is often something else that is mossy, if you give it time enough, to wit, a grave. The medicine and the disease are too much for the poor fellow, and between them he comes to grief and "goes to grass." Venture to suggest to this vendor of antiquities the virtue of good nursing and nourishing food, and incessant watching that nature has fair play, and he denounces it as the wisdom of old women which is foolishness with mummies. The doctrine is, better die according to law than live according to grandma! The physician who studies his patient like a new book; who reads his peculiarities as if they were in print; who sees wherein this case differs from any other; who recognizes the fact that man is not a stereotype, and who finds his treatment less in the pink-and-senna scented library than by the bedside; who dares prescribe what he thinks rather than what he remembers; who believes that books record other men's experiences, and can be verified or condemned only by his own,—this man can never be a man of grooves.

THE TEACHER.

The most useless of stupidities is the teacher who is a groove-runner; who has swallowed text-books without digesting them, and feeds his pupils with the morsels as old pigeons feed squabs, until, like himself, they are all victims of mental dyspepsia, which is a curious synonym for education. Children subjected to such diet are as likely to get fat and strong as so many grist-mill hoppers, that swallow the grain without grinding the kernel. Such teachers forget that one, like Judith's sister "Feeble-Mind" in Cooper's novel, may have a prodigious memory. Who has not known a fool who remembered everything he heard and just as he heard it, who could run up and down the multiplication-table like a cat upon a ladder, and rattle off rule after rule without missing a word, and that was all there was of it—he was a fool still? A good memory built into a well-made intellectual structure is a noble blessing, but that same memory with nothing to match it is like a garret without any house under it; a receptacle of odds and ends, that are worth less than those papers that losers of lost pocket-books are always advertising for, "of no value except to the owner."

Take English grammar under the man of grooves. Learning to swim upon kitchen tables, buying a kit of tools and so setting up for carpenters, are all of a piece with his grammar. Hear them defining a prep'-sition as "connecting words, and showing the relation between them," when not one pupil in a hundred ever finds out whether it is a blood relation or a relation by marriage. Hear them parse: "John strikes Charles. 'John' is a noun, masculine gender, third person, because it's spoken of, sing'lar number, nom'native case t' 'strikes.' 'Strikes' is an irreg'lar, active, trans'tive verb, strike, struck, stricken, indica-tive mode, present tense, third person singular, and 'grees with John. Verb must 'gree with its nom'native case 'n' number and person. 'Charles' is a noun, masculine gender, sing'lar number, third person, 'cause it's spoken of, objective case, and governed by 'strikes.' Active verbs govern the objective case — please, sir, S'mantha and Joe is a-makin' faces!'" And all in the same breath! What ardor! What intellectual effort! What grooves! Meanwhile, grammars mended, amended and emended, multiply. There are four things anybody can do: teach a school, drive a horse, edit a newspaper, and make a grammar. Meanwhile the same old high crimes and misde-meanors against the statutes are daily committed. This comes of grooves and the lack of a professorship of common sense.

Take geography. The young lady fresh from school, who from a steamer's deck was shown an island, and who asked with sweet simplicity, "Is there *water* the other side of it?" had all the discovered islands from the Archipelago to Madagascar ranged in grooves and at her tongue's. end. "Didn't you know," said the father to his son, who expressed great surprise at some simple fact, "didn't you know it?" "Oh, no," replied the little fellow; "I *learned* it a great while ago, but I never *knew* it before!"

Take arithmetic. Show a boy who has finished the book, and can give chapter and verse without winking, a pile of wood and tell him to measure it, and ten to one he is puzzled. And yet he can pile up wood in the book, and give you the cords to a fraction, but then there isn't a stick of fuel to be measured, and that makes it easier, because he can sit in his groove, and keep a wood-yard. "So you have completed arithmetic," said the late Professor Page, of the State Normal School, to a new-come candidate for an advanced position; "please tell me how much thirteen and a half pounds of pork will cost at eleven and a half cents a pound?" The price was chalked out in a twinkling. "Good," said the professor, "now tell me what it would cost if the pork were half fat?" The chalk lost its vivacity, the youth faced the blackboard doubtingly, and finally turning to the teacher with a face all spider-webbed with the lines of perplexity, and with a little touch of contempt at the simplicity of the "sum," and, possibly, of himself, he said, "It *seems* easy enough, but I don't know what to do with the *fat!*" That fellow was not a fool, but a groove-runner. A little condition was thrown in that he never saw in the book, and that groove of his had never been lubricated with fat pork.

THE CLERGYMAN.

Clergymen are liable to preach in grooves; to employ certain hereditary forms of speech that blunt the edge of expectation; forms whose first words suggest their followers to every hearer, and leave nothing to be listened for. Men should preach in types, and not in *stereo*-types. Words should not be uttered in blocks of phrases. It is dull and lumbering business. The art of putting things is a great art. Truth is old, but then in what numberless lights it may be revealed! Truth is the sun. He shines with one steady, everlasting beam, but behold the glories of refraction, that give the color and the beauty of the world! Preachers should be refractors. They should see the Bow from the mountain-top as well as from the plain. Hope dwells in the valleys, but Faith is a mountaineer. They should sometimes see the circle swept and finished,— the seal of the new covenant complete as the marriage-ring of Earth and Heaven. There is no grooved route to such vantage-ground of view,— such glimpses of glory.

Dionysius, the tyrant, has been sufficiently denounced, but the tyranny of grooves has never been written. Several years ago I spent a day or two in the engraving department of the Treasury. The men sat in rows and in silence before a well-lighted table.

One was at work upon a Pilgrim, and another giving Pocahontas a friendly touch. But what interested me most was this: you remember the fine parallel lines that used to cross the postal currency, like fairy furrows. The lines grew dim with frequent use, and it was necessary to sharpen them by deepening the impression. There sat a man with a worn plate before him, and a little instrument like a gang-plow. He set it carefully upon the plate, and ran it through those miniature furrows. Should he vary a hair's-breadth, the plate would be defaced and ruined; but he struck the groove with unerring accuracy every time. He said, "I hear the tool fall into the furrow, and then I run it right through." I bent my ear to listen, but no sound even as loud as the tick of a dying watch rewarded the effort. To my unpracticed sense there was no sound at all. The man laughed and said, "Neither could I at first, but now I hear it as plain as a hammer!"

Grooves are subtle things sometimes, and a man, like that gang-plow, strikes into them without knowing it, until he can travel nowhere else without spoiling his work. Denunciation of this "cold and unfriendly world" is one of the groove formulas, and some clergymen almost make us fancy they think the Devil made it, and not the Lord, who pronounced it "good." There is another and a better world, but let us thank God for this, the very best world we have ever been in.

> "Life's field will yield as we make it,
> A harvest of thorns or flowers."

It *is* wonderfully easy to talk in a groove. A noted professor of Hebrew went to Germany to spend a year or two in study. One of his associates of the faculty began to pray him on to the ocean before he had left New York. It was a new phrase introduced into his chapel petition, "Our brother on the briny deep." It was the Atlantic ocean surrounded by prayer. And so all autumn and winter he kept that unfortunate man "on the briny deep," like the Flying Dutchman, in all weathers, until when the professor struck salt water there was, to say the least of it, a very *cheerful* cast of countenance among the students in the chapel. And there he kept the Hebraist on shipboard while he was walking Unter der Linden; while he was buried in a parchment volume as big as a trunk; while he was smoking a pipe at Heidelberg; and when he was happily home again, it almost seemed as if it might require a steam-pump to get the "briny deep" out of that prayer.

THE GROOVE LETTER.

The average letter always runs in a groove. It has no more individuality or heart than a writ of ejectment. A letter should read as a good friendly talk sounds, but it seldom does. It begins with a "Dear Sir," when the writer wouldn't grieve himself to death were you sent to state's prison for life. He addresses you through three mortal pages, and concludes with a "Very respectfully," or a "Cordially," or some other thing equally absurd. They mean

as much, these cast-iron beginnings and endings, as a
Bantam's top-knot, or a ringlet in a pig's tail. Why
do not people write as they.feel? Grooves. Women
are better letter-writers than men, because honester.
If a woman despises you, she never loves you in a
letter. Her heart is too near the point of her pen.
There is no more relation between the expressions of
courtesy that adorn letters and the real sentiment of
the writers, than there is between the shingle rooster
on the ridge of the barn and that brood of yellow-
legged chickens in the door-yard.

ENTHUSIASM.

Grooves are fatal to discovery and invention. Nobody who follows them ever ventures "across lots"
for new results. The man of grooves always traveled
the two sides of the triangle in great stupidity and
content ∟ It was somebody else that struck across,
lined the hypothenuse, and discovered the shortest distance from A to B. ◺ The world smiles at and
about enthusiasts a great deal, and upon them a very
little, but it owes them a debt it can never pay, for
all that. Enthusiasm is wonderfully contagious. How
pupils catch it from an earnest, all-souled teacher!
There is a professor of Greek in the State of New
York — may his days be long in the land! — who
inspired his pupils, and made them all wish they
had been born in Athens, and almost persuaded them
to believe that the dialect of the Blest is some sweet

and unwritten Ionic.   His word to his classes was,
"Come, let us be Greeks together."   Though his
children are daughters, he has been the father of
many Hellenists.   The shadows of years have not
dimmed my recollection of those recitation hours he
made the pleasantest of the twenty-four.   The Doctor's enthusiasm kindled the dead Greek into a living tongue, and the Attic Bee could have found
honey upon his lips.   But more than this, his enthusiasm kindled in hosts of hearts a flame of admiring
and grateful memories that will never die out.

ROBERT KENNICOTT.

And how could I write anything about enthusiasm without naming young Robert Kennicott, of the
Smithsonian Institute, the friend and companion of
Agassiz; the boy naturalist, born to observe Nature
and to interpret her to his superiors in age and in
knowledge of mere books, but who was fated to die
away there in British America, whither he had gone
to open a new page for the perusal of mankind.   Before his lip had the down of a peach, he found
"books in the running brooks, sermons in stones,
and good in everything."   Living at "The Grove,"
a few miles from Chicago, he often visited the city
with little discoveries he had made and specimens he
had collected, and almost always called at the office
of the writer.   There would be a knock, the door
would open, and he would begin to talk before he
closed it, and talk his way up to the table, and talk

himself out-of-doors. It was a flower, a bug, a bird, a quadruped. He was full of plans to help others to see as he did. He bristled with facts. His mind was luxuriant. He had a love for natural science "passing the love of women." He read in concentric circles from his boyhood home farther and farther until he read the State of Illinois. He explored its Delta, that queer region with tropic traces, that is bounded by the Mississippi and Ohio. He brought out its plants, caught its butterflies, unearthed its reptiles. No hardship was too severe if only he could add some coveted specimen to his cabinet. Slight in frame, he would be brave as a lion if anything for his darling science could be gained by it. What a companion he would have been for Audubon! How like an infusion of fresh young blood he was to the sober old professors with whom he came in contact?

The last time I met him was in the halls of the Smithsonian Institute at Washington, where he had been preserving and arranging some of his captures. As he conducted me through, and pointed out this and that, with apt, swift words of explanation, how happy he was! By and by we stood amid a splendid collection of rodents,—rats, squirrels, marmots, beavers, and all the four-footed tribes of gnawers. And then, seizing one and another he would say, "This fellow, you see, digs for a living, and here is how you know. And this one couldn't jump from tree to tree, like little Red Jacket there, and you see why,—he lacks a rudder to steer by. And this, you

see what kind of food he must eat, because here are
the tools he did it with. That foot,— look at it,—
made to run both ways, up and down a tree at will.
And here is a shady fellow, loves twilight,— see his
eyes; and here one that is happiest in the sunshine,
and loves warmth, and likes folks if he can keep them
at arms-length." And so he ran on with the texts in
his hand, and, though wholly unpremeditated, just
what he said would have made a delightful lecture.
His mind was brimful all the while.

Poor Robert! Science lost a rarely-gifted son,
whose simplicity of character, gentleness of spirit and
enthusiasm of soul made him beloved in life and
mourned in death.

3*

CHAPTER VIII.

THE NORTH WOODS.

THERE is a range of hills in the county of Lewis, seven miles to the summit, called "Tug," and if ever anything was well named, it is that same range. Had the duty of christening it been given to Adam he could not have done better. It is a short word with a sharp pull to it. It straightens the traces to twanging point. It is as expressive as anything in the language,—*Tug!* This morning I am on the lowest step of this mighty flight of stairs, about two tall church spires above the lovely village of Lowville, that Goldsmith would have embalmed in rhyme had he ever fluted his way into the Valley of the Black River. Stand here by my side, and you shall see a panorama. Before you is a splendid table of green and gold,— of pasture and meadow and grain. It is the table of abundance. Beyond it, the land drops away into the lap of the valley that holds Lowville in its apron. Along the eastern edge of the valley, like a piece of silk braid upon a seam, is Black River, and beyond,—ah, beyond, is the great wilderness in the heart of New York, stretching away to the lake that Commodore McDonough immortalized with the

thunder of his triumphant guns. The rising sun
touches the woods and tints the smokes, and the forests, that were drawn up in black and solid columns
all night long, stand apart, and open their ranks a little
to the bright lances of the sun. You see little square
clearings set deep in the woods here and there, like
panel-work, and cigar-boxes, painted white, scattered
about in the openings. Before you are the great
North Woods, where the panther's cry and the foot
of the prowling bear are familiar as plantain in a
farmer's door-yard; where the rattle of the moose's
hoofs used to crackle like burning hemlock as the
mouse-colored monsters crashed through the wilderness; where wolves, gaunt and gray, made night hideous. As it was forty years ago so it is to-day through
a rugged region of an hundred miles. Colton's Map
of the New York Wilderness lies open upon my knee.
I lift my eyes from the paper, and lo, a thirty-mile
sweep of the original, draped in the mountain blue, is
full before me. Let us climb the hill another stair.
We turn, and the picture unrolls like a scroll.

There are figures on the slant hillsides. You mistrust mowers, but you hear nothing. It is the world
in slippers of list. It is a picture of profound peace,
and unbroken silence, and power everlasting. You
fancy Rob Roy could have stood here when he said,
"Were I to lose sight of my native hills, my heart
would sink and my arm would wither like a fern i'
the winter blast." A few rods down the steep side,
as if it had halted for breath on the Gothic roof, and

would make a new bound and over the eaves in a minute, is a trace of crashing roar and grinding strength ages ago. It is a bowlder as big as a house. It has had battles with icebergs. Arctic bears may have clambered up on it, and shaken their white jackets in the feeble sun of the North. The bears and the bergs have vanished, but the rock remains like a great altar of sacrifice. Beneath the rock are two burrows. Reynard the fox dwells in the basement, and feasts like a traveling elder upon the chickens of the land. It is the Valley of Rasselas. Life is an unruffled flow. People live on into the fourscore and ten. You see a veteran laying stone wall under the blazing sun, and he is seventy-seven. Yonder in the meadow is a man "raking after," and he is eighty. You get your first glimpse of a hay-tedder. It is a quadruped. Each foot has a pair of long, crooked claws. Its office is to shake up the mown grass, and kick it all over the lot. It is as vicious as a mule, and the champion kicker of Christendom. It provokes a smile every time it goes into a spasm. You see a hop-yard and a bean-field. Life in the valley is like the hop and the vine of "Jack the Giant-Killer." It runs noiselessly, and it always runs one way,— left to right is the hop's route. Right to left is the bean's,— isn't it? And *if* it is, why?

Sing of the pines and the palms and the cedars of Lebanon, but grass is the very grandest clothing of the globe. Without it animal life would dwindle to "a feeble folk," and the earth would be a desert. It might have been worse for the ancient king, after all, than to be turned out to grass. The hill counties never have so rich a look as in haying time. Such velvets as the shorn fields show you,— golden green with the touches of the sun,— are never seen anywhere else out of kings' palaces.

Among the most exquisite features of the hill country are the elms, with their Corinthian crowns of green sculpture. They are sprinkled everywhere; — now drawn against the sky and clear of the world, from the top ridge of a hill, and now planted all about in the valley pastures like the columns of temples begun. Oaks are rugged, maples hide whole summers in their leafy recesses, but for airy grace and enduring beauty the elm excels them all. It is the lady-like tree of the woods.

SEVEN LAKES.

There are seven pieces of fog just tangled in the top of the forest. Unlike the article coveted by Jason, the wool dealer of old times, they are silver instead of golden. The writer stood in his boyhood about where we stand to-day, and with him one who guided his uncertain steps. Those seven fleeces were there then! That faithful friend and guide bade the child count them, and then he said, "Those little clouds are a sort of picture in the air. Beneath each one in the depth of the woods is a lake. You cannot see it, but it is there, and it *will* be there,— its silver picture yet hung above it,—when you and I are gone." With that we came silently down the stairs, and the boy longed to be twenty-one, that he might do the first man's business of his life,—penetrate that wilderness and look upon the mysterious originals of those aerial phantoms. One of the twain long ago went away to be at rest, which is far better, and the other is here to-day. There is not a stain upon those untarnished pictures. Like the Clouds of Magellan, they are everlasting. Though the writer has never yet seen the calm and shaded waters, he knows that they are there. He believes those lips that never told him wrong, and behold here the seven witnesses to bear testimony every sunny, summer morning! The lesson of the wilderness is worth bearing away into the thronged world,— the lesson of faith in the things unseen and eternal!

VILLAGE ROOSTERS.

You pass little villages in the valleys. There is a period in the life of small villages, as of small girls, called the "hateful age," when kitchen smokes are distinguishable and instructive;—that woman had fish for breakfast, and this one flesh;—where everybody dwells in a glass-house, and is about as conspicuous as if he lived in a lighted lantern. If you want to be inventoried, walk the streets of such a village, and the pagans will "take" you like a photographer. You'll be a stereoscopic object in spite of yourself. Doors will be ajar with noses in them, and the sharpest eye they have. Faces will be framed and glazed in the window-panes. You will be fairly surrounded by observant pagans. It has occurred to

you how many more people there are in a little
hamlet that resemble a disabled milking-stool, "without any visible means of support," than there are
in larger towns. See the front steps of that village
store, this minute. One, three, five, eight,—there
are nine persons, like the ancient blackbirds, "all in
a row." They have gone to roost, but they are as
observant as magpies. A lady is coming down the
street. Those nine heads, carrying eighteen eyes,
turn to the right and watch her. As she nears them
those heads swing slowly around. As she passes they
are all front-face. They see her from top-knot to-
gaiter-button. Then slowly to the left those eyes
revolve. They follow at her heels like spaniels.
They run up her dress to the nape of her neck like
mice.

When Robert Raikes with his Sabbath schools began upon the London gamins, he commenced with
sermons, but he couldn't get at them. He must un-
earth them first. So he revised his practice and tried
soap and water, got down to the boys and succeeded.
Every such village should introduce hydropathy for
the health of store-door and tavern-step roosters. It
should buy a hand fire-engine, not for the purpose
of putting out fires, but extinguishing *loafers.* I
should like to help man the brakes in some of those
villages where they keep the featherless poultry on
the door-steps!

"RETIRED FARMERS."

Many of the villages in the hill counties are blessed — or otherwise — with the kind of man called "a retired farmer." I am quite aware that I am treating of "the bone and sinew" of the land; that politicians, in their rural raids on the eve of elections, carry the idea that because a man has permanently crooked his back at the plow he must therefore be morally straight as a ramrod; that a soft white hand and a smutty heart are one pair, and a horny, sun-browned palm and great cleanliness in the left breast are another. Concede it all, and yet what business has a stout, hearty farmer to "retire," and sell his home where his children were born and his fields made abundant answer, and go to the nearest village, and get his milk from a tin cow, and buy a rickety piano for his girl, and sit on dry-goods boxes and whittle sticks? That a man who has lived in a stone pen half his days, and had a brick earth under his feet, and a strip of sky a hundred feet wide and half a mile long over his head, should sigh to shut day-book and ledger, and go away into the clean country, and have a round horizon to himself, and a sky not cut in slices like a card of General Training gingerbread, is no mystery. But the hegira in the opposite direction is incomprehensible. The farmer depreciates when he "retires." He is worth less to the world than he was before. The day he transplants himself he has done growing and doing. To

be sure, he underbids the village day-laborer sometimes, and so takes the money out of the father's
hands and the bread out of the children's mouths;
but unless this be a contribution to the community,
he is not distinguished as a benefactor. In fact,
"retiring" is not quite safe for anybody who desires
length of days. About the driest sticks imaginable
are *statis*-tics, but they tell a grave truth when they
show that where a man voluntarily withdraws from
his life-work he is about done living. As a rule,
"he died in the harness" is a pretty good epitaph
for man or horse.

AN OLD HOMESTEAD.

American homes are, generally, about as ephemeral
as a morning-glory, and furnish quite as eloquent a
sermon as can be preached, upon the evanescence of
earthly things.

A home where a grandmother smiles down the
generations like a small, benignant providence; where
rooms here and there all over the house are hallowed
by births and deaths and weddings and contented
toil; where bits of old furniture keep you from for-
getting you were ever a child, and whither you escape
as to an altar of refuge from the heat, hurry and
heartlessness of the big world, and grow better and
younger for it all,—such a home is an ordained
preacher; but, alas, how often, in this land of change,
is it "silenced," and ignobly banished from the
ministry!

4

Just the place for old relics and heirlooms is this
hospitable homestead where I write. "The olive-
branches" are all scattered and gone but one, and she
brightens up the house for the tall father and the
faithful mother "and the stranger within the gates."
Just the place for hair-trunks, red, brindled and white,
and worn in spots as if they had been chafed by a
harness; trunks trimmed with brass nails, and lettered
upon the cover with the same "O.S.," which may well
mean old style, for lack of a better rendering. A little
hand-trunk, about the size of a large woodchuck, is
brought out, girt with a little leather strap. It is
older than reader and writer together. It is fat with
papers going back into the babyhood of the century.
Here is the colonel's commission, signed by a dead
governor, attested by a dead secretary; and here
another, showing his right to be called captain; and
there, close by war, is love! Here is a woman's writing, neat and regular, wherein she berates him in
quaint verse for his attentions to another girl. Girl?
Bride, mother, dead, dust, near half a century ago!
And here is the rhyming answer, on yellow paper
withered as an autumn leaf. But they kissed and
were friends. Just the place for old daybooks and
ledgers. Here are fifty pounds of them, written in a
hand as plain as a guide-board. Pages covered with
the names of dead men and dead women that were
transferred, many a year ago, to gray slabs and marble
monuments among these mountains, and away to the
West where the red skies promise a glorious morrow;

accounts for ribbons and calico of patterns as dead as
the Pharaohs. We turn the big books back beyond
the $ Cts. Mills, of Federal money, and here we are
among the £ S. D. of the old world!

The sight of these relics quickens the memory,
and stories are passed about, the latest of which is
no chicken, not one of them being less than twenty-
five years old. The faithful wife and mother, younger
at sixty-nine than the Dolly Vardens of a single score,
brings out the cards with which she won many a game
aforetime. A pair of aces with handles to them is that
" lone hand " of hers — a brace as mysterious to modern eyes as anything unearthed at Pompeii, for they
are the old-time tools for carding wool. And so the
talk and the show run on, giving glimpses that grow
rarer every year of the sturdier times, when the
Adams " delved " and the Eves " span "; when men
fought wolf and wilderness, and women marched
abreast with men.

Almost every old house among the mountains is
haunted by gray-headed stories, as jolly as so many
sparkling Octobers. You can hardly stand by the
grave of a pioneer where a laughing anecdote does not
mar the solemnity of the weedy and silent place.

But our rambles in the woods are ended for the
year. As an Irishman might be charged with saying,
wood is one of the most precious of metals. " From
the Ark on Ararat to the Cross on Calvary," wood
has been instrumental in the salvation of two worlds.
Did you see the precious woods in the Brazilian de-

partment at the Centennial? The clouded marbles right from the tree; the rose-tinted, amber-colored surfaces, just as they grew, ranging almost from ebony to alabaster, and richer than any work of art?

But to me there is no more beautiful wood than the hard maple, the rock maple, the sugar maple, that sweetens thought with memories of the bubbling kettles in the faint-blue, smoky woods, with the soft April moon over the right shoulder, and the promise of resurrection showing here and there in the leafy loam at the edge of the snow-drifts; and the little camp with its roof of mighty barks and its couch of hemlock boughs; and the early eggs tumbling about like dolphins in a baby kettle of sap; and the girls chattering by the fire, seated upon a divan of straw; and the men looking like quaint pictures of "Libra the Scales." But the maples are down, and so are the patient wearers of the wooden yokes, and so are the girls, and a trampled street runs over the site of the camp-fire, and corn waves and gardens smile where squirrels and vines ran up and down the rugged maples at their own sweet will. If memories are deathless, as some men think, then there will be stray recollections of the sugar-bush where they sing the New Song.

But beyond the flavor of the maples is the sight of them; now, when they roll up their clouds of green in the summer, and now, when winter has blown away the leafy tempest, and the trees are logs, and the logs are cleft, and built up in the old fireplace, and the splendor of fire takes possession of the log hut fit for rabbits to hide in, and the rudeness becomes radiance, and the homely heap a palace.

I have a looking-glass that has had in it a whole generation of shadows, and the frame of it I saw in the living tree, and it was as full of birds'-eyes as a pigeon-roost in full feather; and there is a maple ruler somewhere that a leaden plummet followed when I drew lines to write "compositions" by, about "Spring," and "Health," and such things: an implement that was applied sometimes to my open palm in a warming, if not a welcome, fashion; and that ruler is as full of curls as the head of a golden-haired Saxon, and about the color of it. Ah, South America is gorgeous, but North America is glorious!

CHAPTER IX.

FUNERAL EXTRAVAGANCE.

THE OLD GARDEN.

IT was a long time ago, but the picture is plain as yesterday. A little village like a bird's nest among the leaves. A house, low-browed and double-chimneyed, where lilacs blossomed by the door-stone, and roses looked in at the green window-panes. On one side, an orchard with robins and seek-no-furthers — they used to call them signifyders? On the other, a garden with a broad walk down the middle, bordered with pinks and garden sorrel, four-o'clocks and nasturtiums. There were columns of carrots and battalions of beets and companies of parsnips and regiments of onions, and a row of cabbages, a squad of green recruits, all stupidly standing, wrapped in their voluminous ears, awaiting orders. There was a sort of general's staff of sweet-corn in a corner, all with drawn swords and tassels of silk; and a plumed troop of asparagus in the rear; and a picket line of damson-plums and currant bushes along the fence. There were sage and summer-savory in their little beds, while an Indian tribe of painted poppies drowsily camped among the families of dill, caraway and coriander, for

Sitting Bull was not yet. Watermelons green as
an earth with perpetual summer, and muskmelons
marked like an artificial globe with meridian lines,
and conical-shot of cucumbers that were trying their
best to be cactuses and soured into pickles at failing,
composed the garden artillery, while peas in white
favors that carried plump knapsacks of green, and
their cousins the beans, those pets of the Fabii, that
climbed the poles with the agility of Darwin's own
private grandfather, made up the commissary corps of
the garden. The balmy shadow of a great Gilead fell
upon the path by the gate and sweetened all the air.

THE BOY'S FUNERAL.

In the little door-yard were two Lombardy poplars,
married by a grape-vine that aproned its clusters and
swung over the path and shed sun and rain like a
roof. In that shadow on a summer's day stood a tea-
table, with a coffin of cherry upon it, and just as
much silver about it as a chrysalis has. Upon a little pillow within lay the head of a dead boy — verily,
a pillow of perfect rest — one of that countless multitude of whom the Savior had said, "Suffer little children to come unto me, and forbid them not." I am
afraid the mother disobeyed and forbade, but the child
heeded the invitation and went.

The neighbors stood reverently around, the minister beside the coffin. He read a chapter; said a few
words to "the mourners," as was the fashion of the
day; he told us all to be even as little children, and

invited us all in the name of the Master. And then
"they sang a hymn and went out," as the disciples
did from the supper — out into the yellow road, and
away to the grave-yard. There was no plumed hearse,
that carriage for one, and glossy as anthracite out of
the mine, but only "bearers." All walked but the
aged, the feeble and the dead boy. The grave-yard
was as full of gray slabs as a quarry, and they leaned
this way and that, and bore dates that went back into
the seventeen hundreds, and texts of scripture, and
quaint little couplets that limped into the grass and
crept under the moss and were lost. They were the
very "sermons in stones" of the old play. Some family graves were like the strings of David's harp,—
father, mother, children, side by side. But summer
was doing its best to cover everything up with luxuriant life.

Beside the gate stood a bier,— a lean, black frame
with four handles. It stood there winter and summer, always waiting, always ready. Some seasons the
grass grew up rank and tall around it, as if to hide
the thing from passers-by, but it never could be lost.
Death was sure to find it. And so the boy was buried
out of sight. All was done decently and in order.
The funeral was not a ceremonial, but a simple, neighborly, loving service.

SETTING OFF DEATH.

I do not mean to say that in these crowded times
any such method is possible. I have no grudge against

the undertakers, and the makers of caskets, and the drivers of mourning coaches, and the ostriches that lend their feathers; but I do mean that the ostentatious and the rich are setting a deplorable example to the world. Nobody of ordinary means can afford to die, or at least to be buried, at present prices. It is a piece of extravagance not to be indulged in. It is something strange how it comes to cost so much to get into the world before you have begun to be of any use, and to get out of the world after you have ceased to be of any use.

I mean to say that the extravagance of the age follows us to the grave; that many a widow has robbed herself of daily bread to give her poor husband as grand a funeral as her neighbor's, that he might ride for once in state who never rode at all. A little late for him to enjoy it, the demonstration is for people who never cared for him when alive, and who shall cry, "A splendid funeral!" as the procession creeps by, like dots of shadow in the sunshine; or, if not that, then because she takes this way of relieving her heart and expressing her sorrow, even as the Indian widow sometimes voluntarily sacrifices herself on the funeral pile of her dead husband. And neither of them is a reason. I know of a funeral, only yesterday, of a poor laboring man of two hundred and forty dollars a year, whose funeral cost eight months' wages. It was as if he had cut off the total income of his wife and children in an instant, and taken away with him two-thirds of a year's wages besides. It certainly would have been very unkind of him, if he could have avoided it; he would not have died if he could have had his own way. But the unkindness comes in somewhere all the same. It is fathered upon the public sentiment, fostered by vanity and pride, and not by grief and affection, that a man must be treated better after he is dead than he ever was in his life.

Our Irish fellow-citizens make a pageant of a funeral, if not a festival. They yield to nobody in their demonstrations of respect for the dead. Their processions are drawn out like an Alexandrine line, and their funerals are a success. "Who is dead?" asked somebody, as twenty or thirty carriages filed along the street. And the reply was, "It is either some public dignitary or an Irishman. I'll inquire," and it proved to be a porter in a down-town store! The love of an Irish mother for her children is a proverb, and I must respect the feeling with which she robs herself of the necessaries of life to give her darling what the world shall pronounce a fitting burial.

But, say the objectors, "what would you have? Shall we not honor our dead? May we not do as we please with our own?" And the answer is just this: let the funeral obsequies be conducted appropriately and well, but shut out vulgar extravagance from the severe presence of death. Let not the lavish expenditure of the rich invest dying with two terrors for the poor: first, the dread of death itself; and second, the dread of how they shall defray the cost of the funeral.

FLORAL OFFERINGS.

Flowers are beautiful and significant. Placed in the hand or on the breast of the dead, strown upon the coffin and gracefully disposed about it, they become sinless preachers in whom is no guile. It is pleasant to see a young girl lying amid the flowers she loved,— the flowers that are so like her. It is suggestive to see the strong man shorn of his strength holding a little flower in his dead fingers. How strikingly the likeness of the earthly fate of the two comes out when we see them together! But even this is carried to an excess that calls for censure. Costly exotics are fairly stormed down upon the dead in oppressive profusion. It is a wholesale slaughter of the innocents because one man has died. I have no satisfactory statistics at command, and if I had they would be more unsatisfactory still, but it is safe to assume that money enough is annually expended in this country in the purchase of flowers for excessive funeral decoration, and for princely casket and cortége, to support fifty thousand orphans for a round year, and to fill the failing cruise of fifty thousand widows. And so there is some show of justice in saying that this prodigality produces the suffering it does not relieve.

Somehow the *purchase* of floral offerings for our own dead always seemed to me a little like the paid mourners and weepers of earlier English times. But when these gifts come spontaneously from friends, just as they sprang from the earth, all thought of commercial values is happily banished from the mind. One December day, Lizzie, one of the loveliest girls in all the world, died at Hamilton, New York. She was the light of the household, and a challenging angel that summoned out all the better qualities in everybody around her. I do not know why she died. Does *any* one? It was gray winter weather, and the floral glory of open-air gardens was gone. But flowers came from here and there throughout the village. One plucked the solitary calla-lily she was cherishing for a Christmas festival. Another severed the rosebuds that should never blossom. The windows even of humble homes were bereft of their fragrant occupants, and so they came in hands and baskets — and may I not say, in hearts, withal? — through the chill air, and made all beautiful and summer-like around the dear little girl as she slept. Ah, there was no ostentation here, but a tribute as simple and unaffected as the flowers themselves. It reminded me of that *other* funeral with which I began this article — the out-door obsequies of her far-away uncle, "the little boy that died."

The beautifying of the last sleeping-places of mankind is a noble and an ennobling work. I would not have it diminished if I could. The loveliness is for all, and when poor men and women "take their places in the silent halls," they share and share alike, as do the heirs in an equitable will. Perhaps the shadow of some great man's monument may fall upon their graves, for at last they are admitted into what the world calls good society. Only this: If dying, a man cannot relieve the distresses of the poor immediately around him, and have at the same time the costliest of monuments, let his executors direct that the proposed shaft be shortened a few feet below the original design, and a sculptured angel or two be left out, and the sum they would have cost be given to the poor. So shall they be angels indeed.

A girl on the threshold of womanhood died, lovely, loving and beloved. Her life was like sunshine in shady places. Her resting-place is marked by a plain marble, recording her name and the dates of birth and death. You must look elsewhere for her monument, and you will find it. Her father built a church-edifice free to the poor, and a school-room beside it, and he named them both for her. And finding it, you can take up the inscription for Sir Christopher Wren: "If you would see my monument, look around!"

Let men set forth their tables with a service of silver if they can, and garnish their halls with pictures and statues, and all things of beauty that are joys forever. So far they need not consult the comparative poverty of the majority, or pay it homage; but in this matter of dying, all men and women are precisely equal before God and the world. The burial is a common necessity, and for this reason, if for no other, these barbaric funeral extravagances of wealth should be held "more honored in the breach than the observance," for the sake of those who are weaker and poorer than they.

CHAPTER X.

T HERE is a quaint, old-world flavor about that
Anglo-Saxon word *inne* — inn. Direct, simple
as mother-tongue can make it, the word tells all that
is worth telling. Painted in black letters across a
sign, oval and white as an egg — an anomalous egg,
with little ringlets of sheet iron around the curve —
and the sign set upon a post that *leans* a little, as
if to give the word *Italic* emphasis, it is at once an
announcement and a card of invitation: "INN." The
unhappy William Shenstone, who said he found his
"warmest welcome in an inn," would have understood
it, warmed to it, and accepted it.

"Tavern" is the next homeliest word, with a
democratic touch to it that gives it little favor. Apply it and see: Astor's tavern, St. Nicholas tavern!
And yet, why not? "The old London Tavern" had
more wit and genius within its walls in some dead
day or two than was ever congregated at the St.
Nicholas or the Astor in a round year. The word
brings up the picture of the bare broad table printed
off in circles with flagons; of a mighty cheese, over-
come and sagging with its own richness; of the pipes

86

of clay rolling up the smoke of their narcotic offerings; of breezy-voiced Englishmen and "God save the
King."

"Caravansary"—a tavern for caravans—brings up
a far-away Oriental scene, with a four-footed train
just filing in from the sands. The very word suggests turbans and spices and silver-tailed horses, and
a gloomy court that looms up with camels.

"Hotel" is as French as a frog. It is second
cousin to palaces. It is applied to everything in
America that "takes in" strangers. It means anything by the roadside that promises "entertainment
for man and beast."

"House" is also an aristocratic, almost a royal,
appellation. The House of Hanover, which glitters
with coronets and crowns and magnificent possibili-
ties, may designate a hemlock tavern in the West,
where a tempestuous runner shouts "All aboard for
the Hanover House!" Landlords are often "left" to
give their own names to hotels, and sometimes they
are singularly absurd. A man named Hatch built a
house and proposed to call it after himself, but it
never occurred to him how precisely it would designate a residence for incubating poultry, till somebody
put the words together before his eyes: "Hatch
House." Ming—a name that Dickens might have
invented—bestowed the patronymic upon his house
in Missouri, and everybody about the place fell to
talking through his nose. The big dinner-bell said
nothing but "ming"; a dusty, snuffling affair, jangled

with a wire, called "ming" in a querulous, nasal way, and ming it was until, a few months ago, the old house was burned down, and even then it was ming, for it ming-led with the elements. You cannot *burn* such a name out of anything!

There is a public-house in Ohio whose name, if shouted at any educated and edible fowl less tough and overdone than a tailor's goose, would throw it into fits. Think of yourself following off a fellow who had roared "The American Eagle" at you, and some gamin in the crowd about the depot crying after you, "There goes a bite for the 'Merican Eagle!" If like Jupiter's bird you could clasp a talon on him, nothing but the law against cruelty to animals would prevent your making a thunderbolt of him. American is very well, and Eagle will do, but American Eagle measures too much from tip to tip.

There is a funny little affectation of grandeur in the way of announcing arrivals at modern caravansaries. Thus you read that A. B. has "taken rooms" at the Cosmopolitan. You call on A. B. and you find him in number 196, fourth floor back, quite above the jurisdiction of the State, and higher than you have ever gotten since you took the pledge; one chair, one pillow, and eyed, like a cyclops, with one window; a room as hopelessly single as Adam seemed in his bachelorhood. But "rooms" is statelier, and we all enjoy it except A. B., who skips edgewise to and fro between trunk and bed, as if he were balancing to an invisible partner. But things double

and magnify in an atoning way when he comes to
pay the bill, and finds the footing as high as the
room, altogether a high-toned institution from clerk
to closet.

THE BUSTLER.

I saw him to-day — the bustler. He bustled into
the hotel dining-room — the long, quiet, decorous
apartment where everything is subdued into pleasant
murmurs — and lifted up his brassy voice, so that
everybody looked and felt as if a big bumblebee had
come blundering in, that they wanted to drive out
with the broom. He talked as if he knew more
about conversing with a herd of cattle than with civil
people. And he accompanied himself with a knife-
and-fork tattoo, and took two tines of the latter in
his teeth like a country singing-master getting the
pitch, when the only pitch for him should have been
the pitch out-of-doors. He was a vivacious animal,
and suggested a stall or a pen, or a yard with a high
fence; was as breezy as a March morning, and just
as disagreeable. And how he stared at you like a
bull's-eye! He should have been made to shut up
like a policeman's lantern, and then *kept* shut. He
snapped his fingers for the dining-room girls, as if he
had lived in a kennel, and gave a little whistle like
an impudent wind at a keyhole. What he meant by
all this was, that it was he himself, that he was
there,— that he was made a little first, and then this
world was gotten ready for him as soon as possible.
He is the man to overwhelm the average hotel clerk,

4*

buzz him down and get number 2, while the mildly-spoken gentleman who is not a bumblebee gets number 182, and no elevator. Bustler could do nothing without noise. Had he happened to be a tailor, his needle would have creaked like a swinging sign. I do not see how, but it would. When he drank you heard him. When he ate, his jaws rattled, and you might have inferred from his shaggy manner that he had taken a turn-about with Romulus and Remus, and been suckled by a wolf. I always suspect that such a man had no sisters, in the gentle sense of the word; and that if he had any at all, they were only boys in petticoats.

ADONIS.

The hotel clerk, who equitably parts his hair in a hemicranian way, and waves it out in two pinions till he looks a little like Mercury when he puts on his winged cap and gets ready to fly; who wears white porcelain shirt bosoms and a seal ring, with a stone in it big enough to kill Goliah if little David had the handling of it; who looks you over in a supercilious way, and puts you on the fifth floor back because there is a *dent* in your hat, and your coat shows the ghost of a chalk-mark on a seam or two — this fragrant bandbox of a man always terrifies me. The higher he puts me up, the lower he puts me down. He degrades me in the sight of the bell-boys, the porters, the chambermaids and the office loungers. Even the bit of a bell-boy that shows me skyward, goes leaping up the four flights of stairs like a ship's monkey up the ratlines, and sometimes he is out of sight altogether.

Had I been assigned to room "10," he would have paced demurely before me like a little man, and I should have given him a quarter. Nobody whips a brush out from under his arm, and pursues me and whisks my coat here and there, as if he were seeing how near he could come to it and not touch it, and the reason is that I am the man in "240." Then my bell is so far off and so faint that no one hears it, and, if heard, it gives no one any trouble. It is as useless as a Canterbury-bell with a string to it. Even the waiters in the dining-room have found me out. They know the man from "240," and they treat me as if I were an object of charity. They never look my way, and the ear that happens to be next to me as they pass is always a little out of order. They do not suspect that I am the victim of the vicious geography of that capillary Adonis in the office. But everything corresponds, and when the bill is presented it proves to be on the same floor. It is a high-toned proceeding altogether. What shall be done with that clerk? If there were only one of him, a shilling's worth of halter would do, but who can afford to keep a ropewalk running for the manufacture of halters for the execution of Adonises?

An Adonis refused John J. Audubon, the ornithologist, a room at a Niagara hotel. He stood and lied to him with a regretful smile that the rooms

were all taken.   And it was simply because Mr. Audubon's boots lacked a shine, and the best side of
him was not the *outside* of him.   James G. Percival,
the poet, was put into a sky-parlor in Galena, because there wasn't brass enough in him to make a
pin, and Adonis was a fool.   But then Mr. Percival
would hardly have cared had they assigned him quarters above the eaves.   And when the writer, seeing
his name upon the register, inquired for him, and
explained who and what he was, Adonis was repri-
manded by the proprietor, and the proprietor apolo-
gized to the poet, and reduced him to the first floor
in half an hour, but Mr. Percival just ate his breakfast and went away.   Adonis mistook Lord Morpeth's
valet for Lord Morpeth's self at Detroit.   You get
that clerk's idea of nobility when he mistook the
man for the master, and himself for a gentleman.
But all hotel clerks are not Adonises.

A BORDER TAVERN.

Were you ever a guest at a border tavern?   The
landlord is a tall Kentucky hunter.   Blooded dogs —
lean, liver-colored, and as full of points as a hedge-
hog — lie gaping about the floor, or hunting in their
dreams with yelps that die in their throats.   A peddler enriches the animal kingdom; one of those fellows that possess all a blue-jay's impudence and none
of its beauty.   Some rough fellows just out of the
golden mountains, breeched in buckskin, frocked and
belted; a knife in a leather sheath, depending like

Macbeth's ghostly dagger, "the handle toward my hand"; tangled and tawny, as to beard and hair, as the tail of a motherless colt on a burry common, snuffing the supper, pace the piazza with the springy gait of tigers before feeding-time. At the first click of the supper-room door latch there is a plunge of the sharp-set crowd for the tables, one or two being just too late for a plate, and turning their surly faces toward the board as they retreat, to wait their turn, with much the expression of a little dog driven away from a coveted bone by a big one. And this brings me to say that if you are going a journey in regions where it is "first come first served," the most serviceable piece of baggage you can take with you is a *woman*. If you have none, then *marry* one, for you are not thoroughly equipped for the road till you do. When dinner is ready you follow in her blessed wake, and are snugly seated beside her and exactly opposite the platter of chickens, before the hirsute crowd, womanless as Adam was till he fell into a deep sleep, are let in at all. There *you* are, and there *they* are. You twain-one, with the two best chairs in the house, served and smiled on. Look down the table at the unhappy fellows, some of them actually bottoming the chairs they occupy, and the arms and hands reaching in every direction across the table like the tentaculæ of a gigantic polypus. When night comes, it is not you that shift uneasily from side to side on the bar-room floor. If there is any best bed she gets it. More than all this, a woman keeps you "upon your honor"; you are pretty sure to behave yourself all the way.

The conclusion is as strong as a lariat, that traveling bachelors have forgotten something, and that if a woman hears a man sneer about her troublesome sex, and their inevitable band-box, and then in some weak moment he says to her, "Will you?"—an she be wise she will be cautious. Men are not a tithe of the help to women on a journey that the latter, in their modesty or their ignorance — I beg pardon, *which?* — are always conceding. Blessed be nothing! A lone woman *can* make the transit of the American continent like Venus crossing the sun, without either insult or danger.

THE OLD LANDLORD AND THE NEW.

Honest and thoroughly English words are landlord and landlady, and used to fit what they were meant for, like Alexandre's glóves. They name a pair of bread-keepers and loaf-givers who feed travelers. In fact, in a nice, white wheaten sense, they are a brace of loafers. But in pretentious hotels the landlady is about as nearly extinct as the mastodon. She has been succeeded by the housekeeper. The landlord is not utterly abolished, but he is often gilt-edged, bound in Turkey and profusely illustrated. No longer does he carve the succulent pig and the noble roast. No longer do the fowls, breasted like dead knights in armor on a monument, fall to pieces beneath the dexterous hints of the carving knife. No longer,

when the guests are served, does he wash his hospitable hands in invisible water before their eyes, and
wish that "good digestion may wait on appetite, and
health on both." He is succeeded by a clerk and a
steward.

In the dining-room swarm a head-waiter and his
underlings in black and white, to wit: faces and
aprons, who stand behind your chair and regard your
organ of self-esteem and look down the back of your
neck, and watch your fork and your spoon and your
plate and yourself, and never wink once. When *you*
have done *they* have done. They know you as an
omnivorous animal *ab ovo usque ad mala* — from the
egg to the apples. No need to say or sing, "Get
thee behind me, Satan," for that is the mischief of
it: he is there already and all the time.

The first landlord I ever saw is but just dead, and
he was an old man in the beginning — *my* beginning.
He kept a stage-house on the old State Road, as far
north as the Black River Country. It was an old-
time inn with a long, low, hospitable stoop, pulled
down over the lower row of front windows like a
broad-brimmed hat, a world too big, fallen over an
urchin's eyebrows. Along the wall beneath this stoop
was a hospitable bench. Within the wide door was
the bar-room, with a great hospitable Franklin and
chuckle-headed andirons with slender crooked necks
craning away from the maple logs as if they were
afraid of burning their brains out. Across the room
from the fiery cavern was "the bunk," a seat by day

and a bed by night. Above it hung a stage-driver's whip, with an open-mouthed tin horn in the act of swallowing the handle, and the stock coiled about like the hapless Laocoon by a long and snaky lash with a pink-silk tail. Beside the whip a shaggy overcoat, a long red muffler, a buffalo robe, and a tin lantern tattooed like a Polynesian. Upon the wall the tatter of an old menagerie show-bill, where a spotted leopard, partly loosened from the plaster, wagged his tail in a strangely familiar way in the little breaths of air from the ever-opening door. But the marvel of the place was the bar — a cage of tall, sharp pickets, and within it "black spirits and white, blue spirits and gray." In the fence was a wicket window that lifted like a portcullis; and upon the little ledge beneath it a half-grown tumbler of green glass was set forth, and a portly decanter of some amber liquid, wherein rolled lazy lemons or cherries, or sprigs of tansy a little pale from drowning — or a blood-red port that came across the sea, or something bluish from the Indies. "Crusaders" were not yet.

In the dining-room there were no sable waiters, and no bills of fare with impossible combinations of letters naming improbable things, but good and abundant food — sugar that looked as if it had been quarried, and white as Parian marble; pure coffee fit for Turks, and tea for mandarins; and withal a hearty welcome. When bedward bound, a pair of sheepskin slippers were produced from a closet in the bar, and "the brief candle" that Shakspeare mentions, and you were shown to a bed fat as Falstaff, to which whole flocks of geese paid feathery tribute. Mattresses were not yet.

That first landlord was a hero to me. He linked the small village to the big world. He was to strangers what the mayor is now. He extended them the freedom of the city for two shillings a meal. There were shillings as well as "giants in those days." By the way: when an American tradesman tells you an article is a shilling, knowing that a single shilling is a fiction and a delusion, he is joking at your expense, and lacks but very little of being an honest man, for he comes within half a cent of it!

5

CHAPTER XI.

CARAVAN.

IT was from that old village stage-house the writer went abroad,— to Bengal, Asia, Africa and the Brazils,— went and returned the same day! Attached to the inn was a shed for the sheltering of farmers' horses on rainy days and Sundays. Through that shed wide doors opened into a stable-yard, walled in on all sides by barns. In that yard the Caravan was exhibited. Think of that, ye Barnums and Forepaughs of the four-footed and far-fetched! The ring for the pony and his smutty-faced Darwinian rider was tan-barked off in the middle of the small area; the cages were drawn up around like a corral; the elephant was in the great barn, with a chain about his hind-foot, marking time, but never marching, after the manner of chained elephants, and feeling through the cracks between the loose boards overhead for stray wisps of hay. And so, for a silver shilling, I went to foreign lands.

Everybody has a golden age. It is childhood. Mankind and poultry are alike,— both happiest and tenderest when spring chickens. In the golden age happiness is the cheapest thing going. You have seen the time you could buy it for sixpence, and have change coming. I have bought perfect bliss for a cent. It *looked* like a basswood whistle, but it *was* bliss. The E-flat bugle of that lark among players in the Marine Band at Washington never sounded half so sweet to me as that bit of piping basswood. The day I am writing of, happiness cost one shilling, and every village boy got the worth of his money.

There was a hyena that looked a little like a famished and angry hog, with a hoarse, rough snort, like a saw-mill. He snapped at the keeper when he touched him with a rawhide; snapped when he gave him his dinner. In fact, the keeper said the creature could act more like a human being than any other beast in the Caravan. Ingratitude generally goes on two feet, but here it had taken to all fours, and turned quadruped.

THE HEAD KEEPER.

The head keeper inspired us with great respect, and we thought he had captured the beasts with his own hand. He had a red face, and a loud voice with a brogue and an R in it. When he roused a great fellow in a striped jacket he said, "Ladies and gentlemen, this is the R-royal Bengal tiger-r of Asia, nine year-rs owld," and the subject of the biography gave a growl. "He is car-rnivor-rous and cr-ruel as the gr-rave, and is said to have devour-red sever-ral women and childr-ren in his native jungles. He was taken when full gr-rown and 'subdued with r-red hot ir-rons." Here there was a sensation in the audience, and the tiger swung open his jaws that creaked in the hinges with a sort of rusty growl, displayed a set of cutlery, and gave a great yawn, as if he were tired of the account of himself. But then he had heard it before, and we never had. It was all new to us, and horrible and good!

THE LIONS.

And so the keeper made the tour of the monsters of foreign lands, and threw us little ragged scraps of Goldsmith's Animated Nature, much as he fed the animals after a while with poor beef. He stirred up the lion, and when Leo shook himself and stood up on his feet, what with his imposing front lighted with two great yellow eyes, his mighty mane, and not much of any *body* to back it up, he looked like a four-footed head. Nature took so much pains with the hair that she seems to have hurried the work and brought the beast to a premature end. That hair not only saves the lion from contempt, but inspires respect for what would otherwise be a much exaggerated and unpleasant cat. Touched up and rounded out, here and there, with abundant curls, the color of Petrarch's Laura's tresses, he looks stately as a full-wigged lord-mayor of London, and wise enough to sit upon the Queen's Bench.

The young lion of Timnath that Samson unhinged, if we may believe the old Bible picture, and made a

bee-hive of, and propounded the first recorded riddle
thereon, "out of the eater came forth meat, and out
of the strong came forth sweetness," and offered everybody two and a-half dozen shirts if they found it out
in a week,—that lion was put to the next best use
that lion could possibly be; the *very* best being to
catch him and cage him and show him to boys!
Rampant, he shows well on royal arms. As an em-
blem he is splendid, but personally he is unwholesome
and discreet. When the ass masqueraded in a lion's
skin, he had the best of the beast on his shoulders.

There are several kinds of lions the keeper never
named. There are the lion of St. Mark, and Gustavus
Adolphus the lion of the north, and the Cape of Good
Hope the lion of the sea, and Richard Cœur de Lion,
and Æsop's lion that the mouse befriended, and the
British lion. The keeper had only one variety, but
he made the most of him, for he let him begin to
swallow him, by putting his head into the beast's
mouth, and he bade him roar. A sound like a wind
in a cave sent a chilly wave down our unaccustomed
spinal marrows. Somehow we seemed to hear it with
the "small of the back!" Then the man looked as
complacent as if he himself had done the roaring,
and our nervous start gave him great delight, and we
were glad because we had been scared, and so everybody was satisfied. There are many lions not dwell-
ing in deserts and not kept in cages.

Then the keeper thrust his whip into the leopards' cage, and they leaped over it to and fro, to and fro, as lightly as a yellow-bird flies over a currant-bush. How gracefully they walked, with a long free stride, as we think Apollo walked when he went forth for a little archery practice. They purred like the hum of a little wheel, and their fawn-colored fur was dotted off with clusters of black cherries, and their throats were as white as a lady's chemisette, and their long, fine whiskers were just a stealthy touch longer than their bodies were wide, so that what the feelers could not clear the bodies wouldn't try to. The velvet in the foot and the nerve in the whisker told what they were made and meant for! There are folks, whose family name is not leopard, with the sensitive mustache and the still step. They never make a bold break, but go feeling noiselessly about. The best way to trust them is to make a Thomas of yourself and doubt them.

About feet: forget a mule's ears and look at his feet. No Arabian barb ever had a foot so small and lady-like. It is as handsome as a sea-shell. There is a belief that small feet do not naturally belong to large understandings. They say that great men almost always have large feet, though large men often get about in "number fives." However this may be, there is something lacking in a hale, hearty man who goes shuffling about the streets in slippers, and I don't think it is leather. A Christian boy's first manly aspiration is boots.   Ethan Allen would hardly have chucked Ticonderoga into his game-bag just by asking for it.   It was less a question of battle than of boots and breeches.   What could the bare-footed, Highlander-legged commander of the rugged old fortress do, when summoned, but surrender and dress himself?   He might have been brave as several Cæsars, but what if Allen had trodden on his toes with those jack-boots of his!   Figuratively and liter-ally, a man is manliest in boots.   You hear his com-ing; the firm, unmuffled step.   His trail is not dim, like a savage's.   He makes a legible track.   There is nothing of stealth or long whisker or velvet feet about him.   In nature and in name he is not a leopard.

THE ELEPHANT — THEN AND SINCE.

Then the big barn-doors were opened, and an ele-phant,— it was Romulus or Columbus or Hannibal,— was led forth by a man armed with a pike-staff, and all the boys held their breath.   Two dusty leather aprons without strings were hung each side of his head for ears, and two small crevices for eyes were punctured in the smoky plaster dead wall of his countenance; and he carried a couple of tusks at trail arms in front of him, and his tail depended like a bell-rope behind him, and the general expression of his body was that of an overgrown outdoor oven, and he went around the ring in a make-haste-slowly, sham-bling way.   Then he knelt, and his backbone was lined with little boys as thick as they could stick, and he got up, a fourth at a time, and when he was all up and had given the fellows a short ride, he was commanded to shake them off. The ashen hide, rigged upon rollers, apparently, for the sake of equalizing the wear, rolled around him a couple of times at the word, and those boys fell off like apples from a clubbed tree, and scudded back into the crowd like quails into tall grass. Then the keeper lay upon his tusks, as in an ivory cradle, and was rocked up and down in an airy and oriental way. Last, we were told about the elephant's sagacity and tenderness and general loftiness of character, and a number of other qualities that he never was guilty of, and the creature spoke for himself and lifted his trunk and trumpeted, and shambled back to the barn and drank a barrel of water. We have all seen the elephant since. Some of us have had one, and it has generally proved the most costly and worthless of all our possessions. An elephant in the parlor has been known to eat up the owner's kitchen and credit. An elephant in the state has beggared the people. An elephant of a doctrine in the church has given it more trouble sometimes than all the religion it could muster. Elephants generally are architecturally Gothic and spiritually Goths.

THE MONKEY.

The charm and wonder of the day came last. Into the ring dashed a Shetland pony, all mane and tail and lively as a grig, and upon him "Captain Jack,"— not the Modoc, but the monkey. The sooty-faced burlesque was in uniform of a curious combination of cut and color, for while the coat was a wide-flapped old Continental affair, it flared as red as a British trooper's jacket, and the tip of a tail showing below the skirt behind gave a sinister, not to say satanic, touch to his figure. Upon his head, that bobbed about like a cocoanut in rough water, was a cocked hat with a feather in it. And this fellow handled the reins and stood erect upon the saddle, while the master's whip cracked like a pistol, and around the ring the pony buckled, and the bugles blew and the drums rolled, and the crowd shouted and everybody was pleased and nobody was ashamed to show it. Monkeys are just as popular and quite as absurd as they ever were, but people regard them covertly, out of the corners of their eyes. "Captain Jack" has ceased to be a hero. How we all envied that monkey the possession of the pony! I think we could have mustered a dozen boys who were in doubt whether they would rather have the monkey without the pony, or *be* the monkey and *have* the pony! For three months we all "played caravan" on Saturday afternoons. We were tigers, lions and leopards by turns. The biggest of us made poor elephants, while the most of us were fleet of foot as the Shetlander; but in *one* thing we were a triumph, for we all made excellent monkeys!

Gone is the old Caravan. The elephant unpacked his trunk long ago, but among all my landlord's guests none hold a brighter place in memory than the guests that halted in the barnyard, for so it was that I went to Bengal, Asia, Africa and the Brazils.

CHAPTER XII.

EXCURSION means getting out of yourself in a hurry. That is what everybody is doing in summer days. A man will make a more violent effort to *rest* than to do anything else under the sun. And it is a luxury because he makes it for nothing, while the average efforts of his life are made for money. When the excursion fit is on, it is not the least like hydrophobia, for everybody takes to water like a duck, —salt water, fresh water, spring water, mineral water, cold water, hot water, and if not water then mountains. He turns into a chamois, and goes skipping among the cliffs. When a man is about to rest, he sits up all night to be ready to go in the morning. He is whisked off fifty or a hundred miles, and trodden on and rained on, and squeezed and punched, and he spoils his hat, and his shirt-collar wilts, and he is half-starved, and he sees water and pays five dollars and is happy. But he has a girl with him,— perhaps an old one, perhaps not. And she wears a white dress and a blue sash and a saucy hat, and her hair flies, and little rivers of dusty perspiration are mapped upon her pretty face, and *she* wilts like a morning-glory.

Trains pass every day bound for Niagara, Chautauqua Lake, Watkins Glen,— everywhere. One of thirty-six cars and half a mile long, pushed and pulled by a couple of engines that looked as if they were quarreling about who should have the train, passed yesterday. It carried twenty-two hundred excursionists, who represented at least five thousand dollars' worth of solid comfort and profound rest. They hung out of windows and piled upon platforms like swarms of young bees upon apple-tree limbs. Their faces were widened out with satisfaction,— they looked as crumpled as tea-leaves, and were as dusty as millers. They had a band with them, marked like a flock of bobolinks, and you heard the trombone growling in his sleep.

"JACK."

The man is always on board who wears his best clothes and his other hat. He looks like a tailor's pattern that has been stepped on in a damp day. His hat is the color of a badger, he has got a cinder in his eye, some heel has had a snap at one of his patent-leathers and left a little semicircle of what looks like teeth-prints, he has lost his handkerchief, and furtively wipes his happy face with a coat-cuff. He has stood up for the last twenty miles. He might have edged in, if he could have found an *edge* of himself anywhere, but he was afraid somebody would offer to sit on him, and he should wrinkle his coat-skirts, and make the knees of his pantaloons look like a couple of stove-pipe elbows. Such people would be

handier if the ends of a kettle-bail were slipped into
their ears, that so they might be hung up out of harm's
way.

"GILL."

There is the woman to match him,— the Gill of the
Jack aforesaid. She is attired at once in company
dress, and company manners. She looks as if she had
been sent to the laundry by mistake,— washed, half-
dried, and never ironed. She pulls herself together
on this side and that with an air, when anybody jostles
her. But then if she didn't want to be squeezed, she
shouldn't have been a lemon.

Yonder is a man in an Ulster duster, whose material once sported blue blossoms. It is linen, and he
is sensible; but then it hangs about him much as
if he had clothed himself in a loose family umbrella,
and altogether he resembles a specimen of unhusked
corn with a withered ear in it. Like Desdemona's
handkerchief, he is "too little." There, is a lady under
a low-browed straw roof, as comfortable to live in as
a maple shadow in a sultry day. Here is a girl with
her elegant apparel pinned back so far that you might
think she was dressed for posterity, instead of the present generation. Had she pinned her garments back
a trifle farther, she would have left home without
them, and worn something more becoming. She has
declined three chances to sit down. But yonder is a
pair in cool, clean linen throughout, dust-proof, and
pleasant to look at as a couple of water-lilies.

THE POETRY OF PICNICS.

Excursions frequently end in that disaster called a picnic. A sublime contempt for comfort, and plenty of spirits, are essential to its enjoyment. The particular brand referred to is "Youthful Spirits." If a man hasn't a boy in his jacket,— if a woman has traveled life's road so long that she is out of sight of herself in pantalets and calico frock, then let the twain read this authentic history of picnics and remain at home.

Quite everybody now is munching something under a tree, that is such a mixture of cake, sandwiches, pickles, and cheese, that it has about as many flavors as that blessed city of Cologne had odors, not one of which was cologne. The munching is diversified by discovering long-bodied ants in the jelly-cup,— ants that instead of "going *to*," as directed in the Bible, you immediately go *for*. Then Uncle Toby's fly, that he sweetly said there was room for, is floating in the iced tea; and one of those darting spiders that out-lines chain-lightning has you by the nape of the neck; and a wood-tick has begun to picnic on that part of you commonly called calf, as if, considering where you have been "left" to go, the tick could have nibbled you *any*where without encountering veal! Then the log where you sit is about as pleasant as a moss-grown fog-bank would be, and a bug has gone into "the fearful hollow" of your ear, and a catarrh has entered your head, and you wet your feet in the boat, and you are so mussed and mottled with two kinds of jam

that you resemble a New Zealander in full tattoo,
after a fight. You wear good clothes and take good
victuals, and spoil them all. And then it rains!
You get under a tree, but, as with a pea-straw roof, it
rains harder there than anywhere else; and you begin
to show out your character by turning green where
you knelt in the splashed grass. But that brand of
spirits sustains you, and the more mishaps there are,
the jollier you grow. In a word, the misery of the
thing is the pleasure of it.

Picnics are sometimes made for the "benefit" of
some good cause, but never of the performers. That
pitiful picture of poor Mrs. Rogers, "nine small children and one at the breast," following Mr. Rogers
on his way to the stake, was a sort of picnic with
one martyr, while in the picnics I write of there are
many.

There is an *aboriginal* streak in men and women,
a bit of undeveloped savage. Thus a number of residents of La Porte, Indiana, went and camped out
for a week in plain sight of the city! It was a sort
of chipyard picnic. Had they been houseless gyp-
sies, it would have been no marvel, but they all deserted comfortable homes, and, like Nebuchadnezzar,
went out to grass without being *turned* out. It was
a little like going to the washtub to fish.

Seriously, there may be worse social devices than
picnics. They let stilted people down and timid people out, for a bashful man is never so bold as in
that well-dressed and well-disposed mob called a pic-

nic party. And then they act more like themselves
out-of-doors in the woods than they do in parlors.
People who eat rice by the kernel with a fork, and
taste things here and there in a delicate way, delight
to return to primeval fingers, and bravely grasp a
drumstick or gnaw some other bone. They act as
live clams do that you keep in the cellar sometimes.
When in the dark they open their uneloquent mouths,
but the moment you approach with a light, click, click,
go the closing bivalves, and they are all snug as an
oyster again. Some persons are clams. It is only
in the shady places of picnics that you really see
and hear them at all. Only there can it be said of one
of them, *clamavit*.

CHAPTER XIII.

THE "NORTH WOODS" MEETING-HOUSE.

I SEE the church,—"meeting-house" then,— in
the village of Lowville, as it stands on the edge
of my life's eastern horizon. It was humble as a barn,
but hallowed as an altar. The pulpit, with the architecture of a grain-bin and two stories high,—they
kept the fuel in the lower one,—was about big enough
for the twelve disciples to meet in.) A broad ledge
ran all around it, whereon the Bible and the hymn-
book had place. Not an inch of carpet or velvet or
cushion anywhere about it, if we except a little cushion of green cloth, plump with the plumage of geese,
and looking like a young feather-bed not quite ripe.
It was as guiltless of upholstery as Haman's gallows.
For a time the Sunday-school library was piled in one
corner. The entrance to it was by a little closed
stairway. The minister went in and up and was out
of sight, for whoever sat down in that pulpit was invisible till he stood up. A bench of unpainted wood
was fastened along the wall for the minister and his
"visiting brethren." And what a shining host at one
time and another have I seen there!—Kendrick,
Peck, Bennett, Card, Cook, Cornell, Galushá, Smit-

zer, Moore, Morgan, Hascall, Comstock, Elliott.   They
make me think of the big trees of California.   They
were few, but how mighty they were!   A formidable
breastwork had that pulpit, and fronting it like a bat-
tlement was the gallery where stood and sang the
choir.

〔My father led the choir.   I can see the wooden
pitch-pipe, with a mouth like a whip-poor-will,— I
saw it a few months ago, blackened with age, and
treasured for the lips that have touched it,— as he
adjusted it to some letter where "mi is in E," or
some other member of the musical alphabet, and blew
a slender note that had a plaintive cry something like
a plover's, and they all "pitched in" and sang one of
the golden songs of day before yesterday, while Sister
Green rose and fell with the notes as she stood, like
a boat at its moorings lifted by the tide.   There was
a girl in that choir from the "Number Three" road
that always matched her eyes with her ribbons, and
the ribbons were always blue.   She seemed to me
about the sweetest singer in all Israel.   Where are
the eyes and the tones to-day?   I fear me those have
grown cloudy and these sad since then.   Let us hope
not.

For some reason well known to my father, and so
I never mentioned it to him, a place was assigned me,
during the services, in that gallery, and within easy
reach of his paternal hand.   I didn't sing.   I never
could sing.   When I *do* sing, I depart into waste
places. 〕 Admiring many tunes, I was never suffi-

5*

ciently familiar with any of them to take liberties
and call them by name, except Yankee Doodle, Hail
Columbia, Ode to Science, Bonaparte Crossing the
Rhine,— is he crossing it yet?— "and such." But I
knew Mear and Old Hundred and Heber's Hymn,
and all the rest of them, enough to love them when
I heard them, and passing sweet did they sound to
me then,— yesterday, to-day and forever.

Just behind me was the bass-viol, played upon by
a Christian man whose memory is yet sweet,— Me-
lancthon Merrill, of the "West Road." That carnal
instrument, portly and florid, was not admitted into
that gallery without argument. Some of the silver-
gray brethren and sisters would have had no objec-
tion to psaltery and harp, and even tinkling cymbals,
for were they not all *Bible* instruments wherewith to
make "a joyful noise" before the Lord?— but that
father of fiddles,— well, they associated it with the
corn-pop measures of Money Musk, and the total depravity of "The Devil among the Tailors," and the
profane rhyme of "Old Rosin the Bow," if old Rosin
was old *enough*.

As I remember it, Elder Blodgett read psalms and
hymns as we are commanded to *sing* them,— "with
the spirit and the understanding,"— read them as if
they were something he loved and believed in, and
wanted everybody else to do likewise. You have
heard some terrific reading. So have I. Witness the
man whom I heard "give out" the hymn, and you
may judge how he read it by what he said about it:

"Sing the two fust vusses and the three last," as if the hymn were a hay-fork at one end and a trident at the other. Perhaps the order of importance in the clergyman's mind should be, first the text; second the prayer; third the praise; last the sermon. Make this universal, and there will be less hustling through the hymn, as a brisk fellow wipes his feet on a husk door-mat.

(In those old days I think there were none in the choir but "professors." But in the Presbyterian stone church up the street,— the Baptist edifice was nothing but wood,— you could not quite distinguish the saints from the singers in the choir, because they had all been sprinkled into salvation in the genesis of things,—"in the beginning.") But I fancy they should have let the sinners sing. It might have been good for them. Praise is next to prayer.

By the way: do you know any civilized places where they have sacrilegiously degraded "Ninety-and-Nine," "Hold the Fort," and "Jesus of Nazareth Passeth By," to dancing-tunes under the thin title of waltzes? I do. To steal a communion service for the purposes of a drinking bout would be a companion picture.

(The beauty of that old meeting-house was invisible to the natural eye. It had none at all. It was as angular as an elbow, and as square as a checker-board. Its frescoes are all memories. The grace of its pews was lent by them who sat therein. Under the brow of the mighty pulpit sat Deacon Bachelder and Dea-

con Moses Waters. One was a fine specimen of a
lean deacon, and the other as rotund as one of his
own Pound Sweetings, for he was the man who
gave me Rhode Island Greenings out of his Sunday-
noon lunch, wrapped in a clean red bandana handkerchief. I see the men and women and slips of girls
and boys, a goodly company, in the garments of forty
years ago. I see green calashes and vandykes and
hats of beaver, and cloaks with overlapping capes like
scales upon a speckled trout, and gowns with balloons
of sleeves, and high waists and skirts hanging like
flags in calms, and low morocco shoes with glint of
buckles, and caps with borders like white moonbeams
frilled. I see the long tune-books fluttering along
the top of the gallery as they opened them to the
tune. I hear footstoves tinkling down the aisle in
winter, each swung in a black-gloved hand by its little
bail. I smell caraway and roses and dill in the summer. I smell *crape* both summer and winter, for alas!
Death "hath all seasons for his own." I hear voices
that have died forever out of a voiceful world. I hear
the simple, fervent, childlike petition of Elder Blodgett. I see the dusty slants of the afternoon sunshine
sloping down through the western windows. I hear
them sing

> Praise God from whom all blessings flow;
> Praise Him all creatures here below;
> Praise Him above, angelic host;
> Praise Father, Son and Holy Ghost!

As the congregation rises, I hear the rustling of garments like a breath of wind in a leafy wood. I hear the Elder with outspread hands pronounce the benediction: "Now may the grace of our Lord Jesus Christ be with you all forevermore, AMEN!" And so that goodly congregation pass slowly out with hand-clasps as they leave the doors. They have almost all gone out of life. The dear voices in the gallery are quite all hushed. Dust upon lips, dust upon brows,—everywhere dust!

And the gentle, faithful shepherd of the old-time flock has departed. "The prayers of David, the son of Jesse, are ended!"

CHAPTER XIV.

WINKS AND WINKERS.

I LOVE an even winker, where the fringed lids come down like little sleeps, and then lift regularly off. Not lazily, but firmly, if it may be said of a thing so delicate as a live window-curtain. It betokens the staid and quiet temperament of a man not easily moved, but when moved, strong. Distrust a man's nerve who, when thwarted or opposed, gives long shivering winks with both eyes, like an ox threatened over the head with a goad. The woman who snaps her eye-lashes as if they were whips will never be successfully likened to "Patience on a monument." Boys sometimes call them "eye-lashers," and that names hers precisely.

My neighbor across the way has a single wink if he is pleased at what *you* say, or pleased at what *he* says. If he utters a smart thing, wink goes that eye as if he had fired off his joke with it, and you happened to see the flash. But it is always the *right* eye. I have just been trying it with the left eye, but it isn't so handy. The lid does not shut down so much like a percussion lock, nor fly open so easily. People are right-*eyed* as well as right-handed. We are conscious that when we want to bore a hole in an obscure sentence, so as to see through it, the right eye is the tool we do it with.

When some people are trying to remember a thing, they give five or six winks as fast as possible, as if they would thus fan the smouldering recollections into a blaze, and then they intermit. They are fluttering winkers.

The locomotive, like the Cyclops, has but one headlight, and I am glad of it. Just fancy an engine with two round O's of eyes side by side, glaring through the night, and trailing its jointed body, sinuous as a sea-serpent, with its shining square scales, and something. like a glittering fin lying along the back! It would frighten civilization out of sight. When a man has two right eyes, and I mistrust very few have, he is about as well equipped as an observatory. He is a telescope of himself. One of the most popular speakers in the State, and one of the wittiest withal, used to lower his right eyelid when he drove an argumentative nail home, and clinched it with a hammer-headed story. The laugh in that eye set off the audience like a spark of fire in a bag of gunpowder. The left eye seemed to be left out of the transaction entirely. I am afraid my neighbor of the single wink is not as noble as a Roman. That one wink shuts the cover down upon all hope of his nobility, and smothers it, but a woman with that lonely wink is — well, *whatever* she is, she is not a lady.

It is wonderful how much you can find out about

a man by watching the way he uses his handy eyelid. When he employs it to hint with, there is a
trace of fox in him. Contemplate George Washington's square block of a face, and fancy his right eye
giving a cunning wink! It would extinguish your
respect, besides half frightening you to death. Vol-
untary winkers are not troubled with courage. A
flap of the lid is stealthier and safer than a swing of
the tongue. There is a proverb, a little coarse and
very old, about a wink being as good as a kick. It
is better, for it is possible to commit assault and bat-
tery with an eyelid. It is cheaper ruffianism than a
fist, and there is no law against it. It is the mean-
est weapon a man can carry, and calls for legislation.

CHAPTER XV.

HUMAN FIGS.

THE people who have reared large families of children without any boys and girls among them are unfortunate. There are such people. A child without any childhood is a miserable little animal, and the poorest compliment that can be paid to a boy — if it is a true one — is that he is "a little man." I have read somewhere — perhaps it is a mistake — that a fig makes its appearance upon the tree a *fig*, suffering no progressive changes except to grow bigger. Once a fig, always a fig. I do not think we want any more human figs. First the baby, then the breezy boy, then the boots, then the bother, then the young man, then the hope of the homestead — that is the good old-fashioned order of development. Not having the delight of sitting under my "own vine and fig-tree," perhaps my knowledge of *figs* is imperfect, but yet I insist upon the *boy*. We do not want him wise and profound and owl-like and right-angle-triangled. What becomes of the precocious children seven or eight years older at their heads than they are at their heels? Once in a hundred times do they

6

turn into anything at all — say into men? Call the roll and see.

The writer knew a boy who never learned to swim because the water will drown,— never learned to ride a horse because horses run away,— never touched a gun because powder explodes,— never played with the boys because he would tear his clothes,— never got farther than "barn-ball," which means throwing a ball at the gable and catching it when it returns. He played that — and they let him — because he could play it alone. In fact, in pretty nearly all his plays he had a "lone hand."

Then there were several "becauses," that were never explained. He never went to children's parties, because——. He never went sleigh-riding with the girls, because——. He never learned to skate, because——. Somebody exclaims, What did the fellow know? Was he an idiot? By no means. He could fulminate Pitt's reply to somebody about "the atrocious crime of being a young man," and repeat "Campbell's Pleasures of Hope," and "My name is Norval." He knew some Latin and some Greek, and a little about Jupiter and the Styx; but the sticks he knew most about were sticks of stove-wood that he piled in the wood-house on Saturday afternoons, when other boys were kicking up their heels in a frolic. Not that he was ever overworked. By no means. He had the kindest father and the most loving mother in all Christendom, but then he was to be a little fig. Boy nature cropped out, and he fell in love with a girl. Of course, like Desdemona's handkerchief, he was "too little" for any such nonsense, and so an extinguisher night-cap was put upon the flicker of flame, and out it went!

Now this boy, as I have heard, was not an unhappy boy. He had a blessed childhood, but the trouble was, he peopled that childhood with things of his own creation. He dreamed in the daytime. He grew sensitive, timid, shy. He was not like the kind of turtle whose voice "is heard in the land," but the *other* sort, that draws its head into its shell and never says a word. He fell in love again, with a woman old enough to be his — aunt, and who thought no more about him than she would think of a tree-frog. He fell in love with — it sounds incredible, and *is* absurd, but it is true — with her black stockings! That color, of all others, in or out of the solar spectrum! He was fond of reading encyclopædias. He read Nicholson's old twelve-volume fellow by the month. He happened upon the article "consumption," and he had the symptoms. "The liver complaint," and that too. The article on "the heart" fairly scared him. His own turned over and bounded about after an unruly fashion, and he was sure he had heart-disease. In fact, he was a chameleon, and took the color of the thing he alighted upon. He had everything that he read human beings *could* have, except, perhaps, a young family.

The dark was as populous as London. The distant woods he longed to wander in, and never could,

were filled as full of fancies of his own make as a
sunbeam is of midges. If he had possessed tops,
whips, trumpets, dogs, birds, squirrels — it is *imma-
terial* what, if only they were material — he would
have had something more wholesome to play with
than idle fancies and vain imaginings. A stray dog
followed that boy home one day — not, perhaps, without certain sly and friendly snaps of the thumb and
finger, for the lad had never learned to whistle — a
small colored cur, that carried his tail to one side
like a helm put to starboard. He smuggled him into
the wood-house, and hid him and fed him, and man-
aged to keep him out of sight, and the boy's mother
aided and abetted, and the dog helped him to re-
cover from consumption and liver-complaint and black
stockings — and was running down his morbid fancies
and shaking them to pieces as if they were chip-
mucks, when, one unlucky day, that dog impudently
barked at the boy's father! The father exclaimed
against the strange dog, instituted an investigation,
condemned the boy and banished the dog, and the
fancies returned and the unhealthy longings, and the
evil symptoms out of the encyclopædia. I have heard
him say that, a quarter of a century afterward, he
often caught himself stopping in the street to stare
after some little dingy cur with a particularly short
trot, and that carried his tail to starboard, and think
of poor "Watch," who, he hopes, has gone with
Pope's Indian dog to some "equal sky." Dogs are
good for boys, and so are robins and rabbits.

THE USE OF USELESSNESS.

A healthful pet for a boy, to be perfectly satisfactory, must be worthless financially, useless practically, and troublesome generally. Indeed, it must be a great deal like the boy himself. Your average youngster cannot be brought to consider a cow a pet, particularly if he has to be a calf by brevet, and do the housekeeping for the cow. Likewise a pig. A fan-tailed pigeon is more to him than a coopful of the most industrious laying hens that ever proclaimed an egg. Unless he is Poor Richard's Boy!

As we go along in life many of us forget something that is well worth retaining, and one of the most difficult things for a man to remember is this one fact he knew all about when he was a boy, viz: *certain things may be very useful because they are utterly useless* — financially. The young robin that opens a mouth with a nankeen lining to its boy god-father for the vulgar fraction of angle-worm he holds in thumb and finger; the pansies that make quaint faces at you from the garden border; the shingle rooster in a macaw's jacket that the lad has fashioned with his knife, taking little slices from his fingers now and then, and with infinite clambering and climbing, and loss of buttons and a rent in his panta-loons like that in great Cæsar's mantle, and peril to neck and limb, has fastened triumphantly upon the highest peak of the barn; the clipper mill on the top of the wood-shed that runs at the wind's will, and faces about to catch it like a distracted devil'sdarning-needle, and grinds no grists and makes an idle clatter; — all these and such as these are valuable because they have no value at all.

Distrust the man who goes about with an iconoclastic hammer at a random swing. It is a sort of "skilled labor" that requires no apprenticeship, and not much of any brains. But, for all that, I should like one clip at the almanac of the immortal tallow-chandler and kite-flier, "Benjamin Franklin, printer." Had he said a little less about silver change in that almanac, and a little more about lunar change, it might have been as well. "A pin a day a groat a year" is true, as pins went and groats were counted, but we do not want to hear it all the time. If industry is really a virtue, then the sluggard's school-ma'am must be about the most virtuous individual in the world. Industry is a wholesome and blessed necessity. Like hunger, it is a piquant sauce to our enjoyments. Of the three men, he who *need* do nothing, he who *wishes* to do nothing, he who *has* nothing, the last is by far the happiest. About three people since Adam's time, whose name was good for much on a note of hand, have made a raid upon riches, and nobody has praised poverty so heartily as he who wrote his eulogy upon a table of gold that he had paid for and was able to keep. But do not let us cover the world with a penny, as they hide the full moon with a nickel. A sordid boy, to whom nothing is of value that he cannot turn into money, is of all boys the most pitiful.

CHAPTER XVI.

WEBSTER'S Spelling-Book is the only American classic. Give way, ye legions of poets and scholars, before the little books that, thick as locusts, swarmed and settled upon the whole land! Webster is to America what Burns is to Scotland,— everybody knows a bit of him. You may quote Bryant at five hundred thousand intelligent men, and not a wink of recognition. You may name Homer to another five hundred thousand, and no more kindling interest in the eyes of a man of them than there is in a couple of bone buttons.

But try them with the old Spelling-Book, battered and tattered. Recall the skirmish line led off by "Baker, Briar, Cider," that widened and lengthened into marching columns, and moved in a stately way through the book like a triumphant army. Bring out a fable or two from the commissary department that brought up the rear of that polysyllabic host. Mention the dreamy girl with the milking-pail, to whose complexion "green" was as suited as the green husk jacket is to the young corn, "and green it shall be!" Do any of these things, and about a million

127

will brighten and smile, and help you out with your
reminiscences, and have a warmer feeling in their
hearts for you than if you had shied at them the
Book of Song, or Froude's History of England, or
Abbott's Napoleon, or any other work of poetry or
fiction.

But why the spell of the Spelling-Book among the
hills? Before me is a horizon knobbed like an old-
time vault-door. Dark and strong and grim as a
prison, it is thirty miles away, and every knob is a
Herkimer hill. Behind me is a swell of ambitious
earth that was *always* there. I love it for its con-
stancy, and fancy it resembles the first pictured hill
that you and I ever saw. It embellished that Spelling-Book, and was called

"THE HILL OF SCIENCE."

That frontispiece is as unforgetable as the mother
that bore you. I am disposed to think the rocky,
wooded billow behind me is the original. To be sure
it has no temple upon its summit, with Corinthian
columns; and no long-haired youth in a nightgown at
its base, looking up at the risk of breaking his neck;
and no attenuated angel pointing the ambitious youngster to the radiant steep, but then the *hill* is here in its
rugged magnitude. The boy is a man, the temple a
ruin, and the angel fled. Was it good Dr. Beattie who
wrote those lines for "us boys" to speak, that we delivered in the round-abouts with two rows of brass
buttons down before?

"Ah, who can tell how hard it is to climb
The steep where Fame's proud temple shines afar?
Ah, who can tell how many a soul sublime
Has felt the influence of malignant star
And waged with fortune an eternal war?"

But then that was not *precisely* the way we said it, but in this wise:

Ah, *who*kn tell how*ard* it 'tis t' climb
The stee pwhere Fame sproud tempul shines effar;

and then the rest of the syllables tumbled over each other like a flock of frightened sheep over a stone wall. And how dreadful it all was about the "soul sublime" and the "malignant star" and the "eternal *waw*," as we rendered it, and nobody to say, "Let us have peace!" But the best of it was that not a biped of us knew what it all meant.

"SPEAKING PIECES."

Those were the days when we uttered morsels of Demosthenes and the frisky Dr. Young and the playful Blair's Sermons, and the Devil,— John Milton's, — and other merry old boys. Do you remember the Belshazzar quake you had, when called out to — make a fool of yourself and the man you misrepresented? How you kept swallowing with nothing to eat, as if the "piece" you were rendering came from your stomach, and you were doing your best to keep it down? Get out of yourself and look at yourself as you stood there, working with both thumbs and forefingers at the two outside seams of your pantaloons; and casting scared glances at the girls, as if they were hungry ogres and you a tender titbit; and hearing something under the left side of your jacket *thud, thud,* like the old-fashioned "pounder" on blue Mondays; and snapping your little bow,—o as in cow,—at the school, and going to your seat as limp as a wet handkerchief. And so America is filled with orators "even until this day."

ELOCUTIONARY COMPETITION.

Writing of speaking: was it ever your blessed lot to give an address at an agricultural fair, or to make a speech at a poultry show? The writer being a practical farmer who makes "bouts" upon foolscap with steel-pen plows, was unfortunately invited to address the farmers. But no sooner had he begun to say something sweet and green about rural life and glorify the farmer, and mention "the sage of Monticello,"—meaning Thomas Jefferson,—which a good old lady, after the address, said she should like to get a root of, if it was any better than the old kind that grew in her "garding,"—"the sage of Monticello" as being a farmer; and gone on and introduced a plowman by the name of Cincinnatus, who had been dead so long that not a soul there present knew he had ever been born,—no sooner had all this been done, than an exaggerated rooster, several feet high in his claws, took it into his head to crow and flap his wings like a couple of mainsails; and somebody bigger and hoarser answered him, and that set off the turkeys and roused the geese and rallied the ducks. Then there would be a lull, and the unhappy speaker would proceed to give some lively statistics from the latest Report of the Patent Office, and be just adorning them, even as little Chester Whites are tricked out with ringlets of tails, with pleasant allusions to the farmers' blooming daughters there present, when a perverse Bantam, a dozen ounces of fowl depravity, would set up an incisive crow of defiance as sharp as a needle, and all the feathered Babel take up the challenge, until gobble, cackle, crow, quack and blooming daughters were inextricably mingled. The girls were fairly fed out to the poultry.

The speaker's appeal to the young men to stay in the country and keep up the fences was seconded by some malicious beast of Bashan in an adjoining stall who exploded all the vowels like a professor of elocution, and certain plaintive nasal Cotswolds went through their *a, b, abs* in concert. But when a touching and entirely new apostrophe to the farmer's house, as being the one place on all the broad acres where the most precious stock was reared,— the boys and girls of the homestead,— and the crowd was just ready to cheer, a creature, with ear enough to equip a small audience with that organ, that had been watching the speaker from a shed near by, set up his hideous, sardonic laugh of two syllables united by a rusty hinge with a creak to it, and threw the audience into convulsions and covered the orator with confusion. It was one too many at once; the biped retired, the band played, and the base-drum drowned out the quadruped.

I called on the execrable Bantam in his coop; the creature that set the feathered tribe cackling through my sentences, and he was but little bigger than a stout robin. Anybody, no matter how diminutive, or how small the type you set him in, can raise a disturbance that nobody can quiet. It must just die out by the law of limitation.

SQUARE STEPPERS.

Two-footed or four-footed, everybody likes a square stepper. Job's horse was one of them. The Vermont Morgan is another. I had a chat with a wilderness pioneer to-day, who is never so much at home as when he is abroad. He has camped out so much with his feet to the fire that he smells smoky. It would do you good to see him walk. Lightly, firmly, squarely, just as much purpose in one foot as there is in the other. His tracks in the damp sand are as even as fine press-work. He has his philosophy of "being lost." When a man is certain whither he is bound, he throws out his left foot as assuredly as he does his right,—the regular militia drill, "hay-foot, straw-foot"; but when there is a kink in his brain, the left foot, burdened with a doubt as well as a boot, takes a little shorter step than the right, and so, in his bewilderment, he describes a curve to the left, and keeps coming about to the place of beginning. He ceases to be a square stepper.

The feeling known as being "turned round" is more painful than a pain; when the sun persists in rising in the north and setting in the south, and the engine of the visible universe is reversed. No reasoning will set a man right and mend his broken compass; but if he will just return to the place where the cardinal points are in position, and then carry the reckoning in his head back to the doubtful region, the horizon will swing around where it belongs, and the man and the world will be as nicely adjusted as ever.

There is a world of left-leg marching in church and state. It has traced the haunts of men with crooked paths, and impeded true progress. Dr. Kincaid, the great missionary, was a square stepper. He struck out upon an unknown and rugged route as if it had been the highway of nations. It was no left-foot gait that took him within ear-shot and heart-reach of the King of Ava. He made a march of an hundred years in as many days. It was a grand specimen of square stepping. Literally and figuratively, the left foot wants watching.

CHAPTER XVII.

THE COUNTRY "CORNERS."

THE BLACKSMITH.

THERE is a smithy at the Corners. All day long, clear and cloudy, I hear the ring of hammer upon anvil, and the sullen roar of the fire. Sauntering over, I enter the shop. The bellows crouched beside the forge, with its long nose — a family nose — thrust in the ashes out of sight. Now and then it lifts its back as if about to get up, but just blowing a long breath that brightens the fire, it lies down again. There are cinders, odds and ends of everything in iron, bits of steel, horse-shoes, and a water-trough full of tongs.

The blacksmith is just picking up a lumbering farm-horse's foot as you would pick up a penny, and he lays it in his leather apron, and cuts and carves as if he made the feet to fit the shoes. Children — *his* children — seven of them, are playing about, and he feeds and clothes them all with a hammer. It is a plain case of hammer and tongs. The bit of ribbon catching up that little girl's hair came out of the fire, and has not so much as the smell of smoke upon it. He feeds nine mouths with a mixture of nails, rings, horse-shoes, chains, rods, bars. For a steady diet, iron and steel must be a tremendous tonic. But the blacksmith has the most powerful of all tonics — the love of wife and children — that keeps that tired arm swinging and that forge glowing.

Let us consolidate the nine mouths to be fed with a hammer. Let us say they will equal one mouth a foot and four inches in width — more stupendous in the human economy than the mouth of the Mississippi. Let the blacksmith fashion a spoon thirteen inches broad to fit it. Twenty mouthfuls at a meal are anchoritish rations for growing children. Sixty times a day that mighty spoon must travel from plate and platter, kettle and tureen, every ounce of it won with a hammer in a single hand. Everything they want and wear is multiplied by the magic number, nine. But never think the tired blacksmith would apply the arithmetical rule for "casting out the nines," if he could. Busy and happy as the day is long, he never murders time. He needs no drowsy drugs to sleep. He drops off like a log when the fire is out and the day is done. He falls into line with Tubal and Jubal, Elihu Burritt, Robert Collyer and "the lame Lemnian," and unlike Vulcan, he is not nine days distant from heaven, when he is busy and all are well. He is a blacksmith.

I listen to his hammer as to a pleasant bell. When I think what it rings for —"Shoes for baby," "Gown for wife," "Christmas gifts for nine, nine, nine" — the clink, clang, clink, grows sweet as the chimes of old Trinity the first time my "next best friend" and

I heard them. It was a calm, clear summer morning. The great roar of the mart had not begun. Then, as we walked together down Broadway, with more years before us than there are to-day, there fell down through the still air, as if from another world, the sweet chiming of the bells in "Life let us cherish." It is the very tune the hammer and the anvil play; and so from belfry to blacksmith, from high and low, the grateful bells and pulses beat—"Life let us cherish!"

Among the things strown about the blacksmith's shop are traps for such "small deer" as mink and fox, and now and then a bear. A trap is a pair of jaws and teeth waiting to catch a *body*. The Frenchman said that a theory is a trap to catch a truth. It is generally the *inventor*, however, that is trapped, and not the truth. Be this as it may, here are traps, and there is yet need of them. Bears are unbearably many. There never were more in the Canton of Berne. They make mutton and pork of what was neither before, within a stone's throw of farm-houses. I think a bear has a comic look, so fringed and ragged with fur everywhere, as if he were made coarse on purpose to be sold cheap, and yet with ears so round, close-clipped and neat, as if somebody had finished him off finer at one end than the other, just for a joke, and then laid down the shears.

The two Old Testament bears, good for twenty children apiece, gave me in very early life a wholesome respect for bald heads *and* bears! So when, in broad day, one of these dogs of Herod came down my favorite ravine for wandering, and crossed the road, the bare possibility of something Bruin has since kept me out from among the shadows and evergreens of the gulf. But enough of Ursa, Major and Minor, lest the bear shall be a bore.

MY FIRST BIRDS.

Here now am I, a small volume of very modern history indeed, and yet I point you to that rank old meadow across the road, where the mower can make an unobstructed sweep, with nothing in the way but timothy and grasshoppers, and I tell you that when on the farther edge of boyhood I remember it a tangled swamp.

Village-born, I was caught out in the country one soft spring evening, and passed it. The fireflies' twinkling constellations had risen above it, and no cloud of forgetfulness has ever dimmed their beauty. Then out of the swamp came strange, sweet sounds, as of many filberts of sleigh-bells afar off, when the wearers strike into a merry trot. The first birds I remember to have heard sing were frogs! Nothing in all the music of childhood and manhood ever impressed me as did the trill of those fellows in green tights, and to this day, whenever it is heard, a feeling of loneliness and sadness, yet not of pain, possesses me, and beside the dead, drawn by a dead man's horse, in a dead spring night of "the long ago," a boy is riding to a home now desolate, through

6*

the gray and ghostly shadows, by the starry glimmer
of fireflies, to the unstrung bells of frogs. I look up,
and the maple is glory and the poplar gold. The
sweeps of rain loosen the frail tenure of the leaves,
and they snow slowly down, scarlet and crimson,
gold and foliomort, to the waiting and patient and
ever-ready earth. "We all do fade as a leaf." But
then, "leaves have their *time* to fall," but "thou
hast *all* seasons for thine own, O Death!"

THE COUNTRY STORE.

Just the place among these hills for the old-time
country store that, like Noah's Ark, contains a little
of all sorts. You look for it at some lazy four-corners, within hearing of an anvil's ring, and the grind
of a mill where the creek plays in a wheel like a
caged squirrel. And you find it, the variety store
of a hundred years ago, where needles and crowbars,
goose-yokes and finger-rings, liquorice-stick and leather,
are to be had for cash or "dicker." In the corner
yonder, stands the spindle-legged desk, behind a breastwork of barrels, and a bastion of codfish criss-crossed,
a big blotter spread open upon the lid, goose-quill
pens, a sand-box and a pewter inkstand within reach.

Here is the wooden bench beside the stove, covered
with jack-knife sculpture, awkward II's like a pair
of leaning bar-posts with one bar, and B's like ox-
yokes. It is here that in rainy days and winter
nights the whittlers, smokers, spitters and talkers gather
in and lay their blue-and-white mittens beneath the

stove to dry; perhaps a village doctor with his saddle-bags and pink-and-senna nimbus; perhaps a country lawyer who practices at the county bar in court
time and the tavern bar the year around, with his
dogmatic way and his tobacco atmosphere. Here
Unions are saved, States constructed, stories told, and
pig-tail gnawed. Here "fore-handed" farmers talk
pig and potatoes, and buxom country girls smell of
peppermint, and warm their rosy fingers that match
their ripe cheeks for color. Here clouds of smoke
from clay pipes float up among the bed-cords and
brooms and tin-lanterns and cowhide boots suspended
overhead. And the stove, with its red mouth close
to the hearth, roars and reddens in the howling nights,
and the black nail-heads in the floor are worn silver-
bright by stamping and uneasy feet. A boy, tipped
with red as to fingers, nose, ears and toes, stands before a short row of speckled glass jars in brimless
hats of covers, wherein lean a few streaked sticks of
childish happiness at a penny apiece, and gazes with
watering mouth that keeps him swallowing in bliss-
ful expectancy.

THE SCHOOL-HOUSE.

Down the road, beside a wild spring, is a stone
school-house with deep windows, and walls like a castle. It is as bare of ornament as a Quaker. Neither
map nor chart hides its walls, blank as the face of
astonishment. The seats are a sort of wooden rheu-
matism — right-angled, hard as Jacob's pillow in the

wilderness, and no angel ever in sight but the school-
ma'am. It is the very bones of the modern school-
house. Now and then I wander there, for much of
the time it is as empty as the cave of Machpelah.
But there is something *human* about it that recon-
ciles me. It smells of old geographies and spelling-
books, and readers with ragged edges like the ears
of "the under dog" in the fight. There is a faint
suspicion of noontime dinners in the notched and lettered desks. There are pellets of chewed paper upon
the walls, like cannon-shot in some old fort. There
are nightmare faces upon the seats, and beasts that
never came out of the Ark, for they could by no
possibility have ever got in, and prints of obliterating
thumbs inkier than Ethiopia.

But the limestone fortress has other uses. Nights,
and Sundays, it is a depot for doctrines. There are
not many varieties of Christians among the hills, and
again there are many that seem rather to delight
in being sinners. But for all this, during the fortnight I have been dreaming and looking nature full
in the face, nature as unshaven, unshorn and unkempt
as a Tunker, there have been seven sorts of doctrine
set forth in the old school-house, to about the same
congregation. Just here I rise to explain why Tunker is used instead of the name by which that sect
is best known. Some time during the past summer,
a grand convention of Dunkards was held in a little
town in Illinois, and no end of papers had it that
five thousand Drunkards were assembled, setting the

Good Templars packing their satchels for a pilgrimage, in the hope of catching some of the flock before
they could get away.

An Episcopalian, two kinds of Methodists, a Presbyterian, an Adventist, a Soul-Sleeper and a Baptist
march in doctrinal procession through the fortnight—
dry, damp, sprinkled, immersed; bringing prayer-books,
hymn-books, camp-meeting songs ; preaching "each
after his kind." What *will* happen to that over-fed
company of doctrine-lappers, going through such a
bill of fare from grace to almonds, and apparently
delighted with each clean plate! "They pay their
money, and they take their choice," but it is the
most religiously-dissipated community extant.

ANCIENT HISTORY.

How would you like to be a volume of Ancient
History, substantially bound in calf or — something
— be *live* history, and go about upon two feet? In
the hill country the chances are good for it. You
can meet a man any day in the street, going about
his business, who will tell you things that he saw
in the year of grace 1800. And it will not be a
man on three or four legs that will do it, but one
who at sight could beat Weston at honest walking.
Nearly every man of them is about as certain to
have a panther, bear or wolf story, as he is to have
a shadow when he goes out in the sunshine. "The
almond-tree" of Ecclesiastes shines here. The order
of the silver hair — thanks to clean water, pure air, sim-

ple habits and a kind Providence — is as numerous
here as in an audience the writer once had in little
Rhody, where quite one-half wore the silver crown.
The congregation looked as if they had been out
bareheaded in a snow-storm, and the flakes had not
all melted. But they were not feeble, tremulous people of the "lean and slippered pantaloon," but sturdy-
legged and full-fronted, and faces so frosty and ruddy
that they made you think of October apples. Many
of them had been sailors and sea-captains, and breathed
salt air, and been drenched in salt water till they
were fairly pickled and apt "to keep."

WHO ARE PIONEERS?

Within a month these young old boys have put
the wilderness all back upon these cleared fields for
me, and built up the woods, and peopled them with
things unchristian and uncanny. They talk as famil-
iarly of 1805 as if it were last week, and they fancy
they were the first settlers. Perhaps not. Man does
his best to make indelible evidences of his existence,
and to leave them upon the earth. Nature watches
him awhile, and then amuses herself with effacing his
records, and sifting fine mould and seeds and leaves
upon his highways, and smoothing over his graves,
and the young forests spring up, cultivation relapses
into wilderness, and the globe is as ready as a clean
slate for a new set of pioneer boys. When the
scouts of civilization first struck northern Indiana,
they found forests that the sun never shone in,

where Indian trails grew dusky in the great solitude. They were the Christopher Colons of Indiana. But one day a surveyor, running a government line, struggled through twilight thickets as dense as a canebrake, and broke out at once into a — vineyard! A breadth of some twenty acres was purple and golden with grapes. Choice varieties from the Rhine, they were brought thither by forgotten hands in some immemorial year. Men had lived here then. Women had sung the vine-dresser's song in this wilderness. Children had grasped the rich clusters with stained fingers. Whoever they were, they had gone. The young forest had asserted its ancestral right to the old soil, and the vines had clung to it and surmounted the tallest trees, and swelled like the great billows of a green sea. Make that surveyor a little later in his work, and no trace would have remained of the children of the Rhine. But for years the new race of "pioneers" bore away in the mellow autumns the luscious produce that foreign hands had planted for they knew not whom. So Nature makes room for the marching generations.

CHAPTER XVIII.

AQUARIUS THE WATER-BEARER.

IT rains! It is the paradise of Batrachians. Batrachians are frogs, and frogs are *rana*. Hence rainy, and there you have a derivation crazier than Horne Tooke's. The waves at Chadwick's Bay come galloping in from the sea like plumed troopers, and the white-caps "show a light" away out to the edge of the horizon. The broad leaves of the basswood by my window droop and drip in the rain like the ears of a meditative hound. Little children are running to and fro with little yelps of delight, and a spare skirt flung over their heads from behind like a squirrel's tail. A woman stands in the door of a house with her arms akimbo, trying to get her eye upon one of them. You have met akimbo people. Their elbows are sharp. They are deadly weapons. Such folks should live in scabbards. If she gets hold of the "one of them" she will make the little midge acquainted with the stern realities of life. Yonder is a rooster wet down to a peak. His scimetar tail is only a single dagger of a feather. He looks sorry. The crow is washed out of him.

You keep wiping the window-panes on the *inside*

because they are filmed with water on the *out*side.
You know better, and so does the man who feels in
his pockets for something that is not in them. Right
vest pocket, left vest pocket, right breast pocket, left
breast pocket, right hind pocket, left hind pocket,
right pantaloons pocket, left pantaloons pocket. He
will stand there and make the rounds once, twice,
thrice, and then whip off his hat and find it there!
He is not logical. None of us are.

Eaves are busy, water-spouts jolly, and gutters con-
gested. There is a splashing in little puddles, a
drumming on tin pans, a tinkling in cisterns, and a
tattoo upon roofs. It is a mass-meeting of rains,—
perpendicular, oblique, horizontal, and no rainbow in
a fortnight! Engines hardly have to stop to take
water!

You look down from your window on two currents
of umbrellas. Forget there is anybody under them,
and it is as queer as a dream born of a Welsh rarebit
at midnight. It resembles a stream of mildewed, animated and locomotive toadstools from Brobdignag.
They drift against each other, then part and float
away. There are sleek silken ones that shine as if it
rained copal. There are great blue ones with a border, and big enough for dog-tents, that move in a
lumbering way. Old folks underneath. They say
" um*brill*." There are faded ones, the color of a Con-
federate soldier's jacket. There are wrecks of fellows
with their slender bones thrust through the dingy
surface,— bad cases of compound fracture. There's a

7

parasol scudding along amid the tumefied dinginess, like a bright little flower afloat on a very turgid current. It dodges in and out among the troughs of the sea. Every overgrown umbrella is a threatening billow. Poor little fair-weather flower, and dreadfully wilted and pelted by the rain. Its owner was caught out. You see a white flicker of skirts as she scuds.

"ARIES THE RAM."

There goes an umbrella drawn down over the owner's eyes. He lowers his brow and forges ahead without minding who is coming. He is as bad to meet as a Texas steer, with his unicorn of an umbrella. Umbrella or no umbrella, he butts his way through the world. Clear the track when you see him, unless you are carrying a ladder. If so, just swing it around endwise and make for him! He is always in the sign Aries. Everybody knows him. When he argues he only butts, and when he butts he shuts his eyes. Intelligent adversary! He is a heavy-weight wherever he is. He might do for ballast, if only he would keep still.

"Aries" does not like flowers. He calls them "posies." A moss-rose bud would be about as much at home in his button-hole as it would in an elephant's ear. He has no taste, except it be a beefsteak taste. His flower is a sunflower. He is coarse, hard, hearty, and he succeeds. What *is* success? Not that I do not respect sunflowers,— those big rosettes with their curious mosaic and Nicholson-pavement of seeds. I think of them in the same thought with the just-ready-to-wilt poppy, and the china-asters and the sweet-williams and the hollyhocks, — the dear old tribes of our grandmothers' day.

"GEMINI THE TWINS."

How many young fellows there are in the street, armed with umbrellas every one, and looking for somebody. Watch the girls dart out of store-doors, and make for cover like startled hares. There they go, arm in arm, like two-thirds of the triple link badge of Odd-Fellowship: "friendship, love and truth," the umbrella lowered modestly down so that their two heads are in the *garret* of it, and drifting very slowly indeed. It is a pleasant day beneath it. Had they been in the ark, — they two, — they would not have thought it rained. Umbrellas have determined destinies.

It rains, and the sea of umbrellas is yet ebbing and flowing. There goes a high stepper. You know it by the way the umbrella bobs up and down, like the cork of a line with something nibbling at the hook. Yonder is a man who walks with his *elbows* when he is in a hurry, for he lifts them whenever he "crooks the pregnant hinges of the knee," just as a horse works his ears every time he swallows. Here comes a glider. The umbrella floats evenly along. There a man carries his umbrella at half-cock. It hangs down his back like a peddler's pack. He hails you. He hails everybody. He flings scraps of talk this side and that as he goes. He is a pleasant friend, if you don't mind that love-token of a slap in the back he is always giving.

"AND JULIET IS THE SUN!"

The clouds "hold up." The sun throws off his wet blankets, and touches up the glittering signs, and the glossy water-proofs that are executed at store-doors, and the open umbrellas swung up by the peak, to give you a damp whisk and challenge a buyer. The little Othellos of bootblacks, their "occupation gone," that have been casting disconsolate looks all day at the splashed leather as it spattered by, brighten up a little, reflecting in their faces some faint fore-glimmer of a "shine." The wet arrow on the neighboring church gives a flash as if somebody brandished it. The crowd fold their tents like the Arabs. The umbrella sea subsides, and the people come to the surface. But the character of the picture is not gone, only changed. One holds out his closed umbrella by the tip of the handle, much as you swing up a rabbit by the ears. Another grasps it around the waist, and carries it at trail arms. A third reverses it, as if he were a soldier at a funeral. Another never stops to button the umbrella, but makes a cane of it, the cambric corners untidily flapping as he goes. But the most miserable of men comes yonder. He has chucked his umbrella under his arm, with the ferrule thrust out behind, like a bowsprit at the wrong end of the craft, and trained at precisely the right angle to put out an eye for the next man behind him, who has no idea that he is charging on a pike. He is a two-footed hornet. Can you think of anything more uncomfortable than an umbrella in your eye? Many a man has had a beam in it without knowing it, but an umbrella, never! That human hornet is a selfish man. His umbrella points out his character like a finger-post. His maxim is vulgar and profane. It is "the devil take the hindmost."

A rainy day is a good day to *see* in,— better than when the sun shines. As to-day grows duller and dimmer, yesterday grows brighter and nearer. We can look a long way into the past when it rains. We remember. It is pleasant. It is sad. It is like the music of Ossian. It is both.

CHAPTER XIX.

HILL COUSINS.

HUNTING health and hunting happiness are alike. You seldom find them where you seek them. They come to you by the way at unexpected times and places. The devil is credited with a great deal of mischief that the stomach is guilty of. Many a gloomy doctrine is born, not of theology, but of cold dumplings and toasted cheese at bedtime. The writer has been looking for strength among the hills where the roads are set upon one end and paved, you would think, by old torrents. He rambled without much of any purpose,—a sort of gypsying,—and he found cousins.

There are three kinds of cousins in America. In Scotland there are forty. They are reckoned by numbers,—first, second and third. In cousins I am specially gifted, for I have sixty, and the most of them are sprinkled among the hills of New York, in the counties of Oneida, Lewis, Herkimer and Otsego. Take them as a race, the average distance between the cradle and the grave is about four miles. They have read the proverb of "the rolling stone," and most of them have gathered moss. Children generally set great store by uncles and aunts, always except-

ing "the Babes in the Woods," whom Robin Red-
breast "did cover them with leaves." When these
are gone, and the year wanes into autumn, cousins
are in their prime. They last till snow comes, and
sometimes into the dead of winter. Hence cousins
are a desirable kind of relative to have. As pomolo-
gists say, they are "good keepers."

As you get older, cousins rise in value, because
they grow scarce, but you must not let very long
intervals elapse between meetings. That is, you must
not wait over twenty years. I waited thirty. The
changes are suggestive. Should you meet a cousin you
had not set eyes upon since "cats wore fillets," which
means "ever so long," do not straighten up into an
exclamation-point and cry out over the ravages of
time. Just consider that you are only contemplating
yourself in a looking-glass made of a cousinly face, and
you will grow quiet as an oyster. When people fall
to telling one another, after a score of years of absence,
that neither has changed, that they should know each
other *anywhere*, swear them and see ! Twenty to one
they are both lying in a sort of harmless, feeble way,
in an attempt to make themselves believe that the
Old Haymaker has fallen asleep in a fence-corner,
with his scythe hanging upon an apple-tree over his
head.

Remember a girl-cousin of sixteen, round as a ring
and fair as the moon, with glittering teeth and voice
cheery as a morning song, and hair that tumbles down
her shoulders like a capillary cataract. Leave her to

time for a couple of dog's-ages, and then meet her somewhere, and if Adam's-apple does not take a start for a late growth in that throat of yours, then you must have bolted the troublesome fruit in your child-hood. You scan the face for traces of the girl that was; you pick up a few scattered features here and there, and try to reconstruct them into some sem-blance of the old-time cousin, but it is a failure. And all the while you are doing this, Jane is busy taking *you* to pieces and building *you* over, and there is a *twin* failure. Then she nerves herself up to men-tion her grandchildren, and you recall a joke dead forty years ago, and so you make the best of it and laugh, "as it were," across the graves of a genera-tion, and bid each other good-by, and this dice-box of a world gives another shake, and you meet no more.

When first-cousins give out, there is a stock of the "second" sort ready to your hand. In fact, kind nature seems to make provision for a fresh crop of cousins as the years go on. As a rule, they "hold out" better than nearer relatives, and "stick to" faster and longer. A brother is a good thing. Like-wise a sister. But we get to know each other un-comfortably well, and live so long in the same house and wrangle over the same doughnut, that unless we are of the good children that die young, there is not much chance for anybody's quoting and saying, "Behold how these brethren love one another." The probabilities of fraternal affection increase, I think,

with the number of brothers and sisters; that is, the
relations among the many are less intimate than they
are among the few. Nobody can endure the steady
stare of a microscope without suffering, if he can without flinching. "The fewer we are the more let us
love one another," is a kind of sentimental twaddle.
Remember Cain and Abel! Consider the Siamese
twins! As a rule, Damon and Pythias are not brothers. We used to read in the first book of Latin a
conversation between a lion and a certain insignificant
animal, wherein the little one taunted the big one
with having a small family. The reply was a cross
of cheap magnificence, partly leonine, and the rest
Roman: "One, but a lion!"

LIVING IN MICROSCOPES.

Writing of magnifiers: a man might as well live
in a microscope, with an eye at it that never winks,
as to be a clergyman. The public turns itself into
a policeman in plain clothes to "shadow" the minister.
His patience is tested, his temper is tried, his indigna-
tion aroused, and he has incessant temptations to talk
tomahawk and forget to be a gentleman. The virtue
of the Toledo blade was not in its keenness, but its
temper; that, though you bent the point to the hilt,
it never flew to pieces. There is no such thing as a
fragment, a vulgar fraction of a gentleman. He is
gentleman *ad unguem* — to the claw — or not at all.
The temper of the blade is the spirit of the man,
and how refined it must be in celestial fire to main-

tain its integrity! It seems to me peculiarly true of clergymen that they have nothing earthly to fear but their friends. They are in more danger from them than from their enemies or the devil.

There are merciful laws for the preservation of game. There are times and seasons when it is wicked to slay it. Clergymen enjoy no such legislation. They appear to be game all the year round. We are quite worn out with hearing of ecclesiastical falls and clerical wolves in woolen clothes. Let the lawyers have a chance, for there are more bones of Little Red Riding Hoods in the courts of the law than there are in the courts of the Lord. Let a physician take a tumble, now and then. Let some merchant be a cataract. Let us not have all the Niagaras rolling down the pulpit stairs. Those people who waste their time in "stalking" ministers are generally poachers themselves.

Back to the cousins: there are few lions among them, and not a mouthful of Latin. Such quail-like broods of cousins in the same nest! Eight, eleven, thirteen, and they kick the beam all the way from one hundred and forty to two hundred and thirty, and as a rule, they pull together. Have you heard of any battle in the Empire State? When two fall out it is a quarrel, but when many come to blows it is a war.

When the Waldenses were made to sing, "For the strength of the hills we bless Thee," it was a true song in more senses than one. They furnished

the Christians with caves and rugged fastnesses as
shelter from the persecuting Sauls. They furnish you
with a more vigorous play of muscle and a freer respiration. Wherever you are in Otsego the horizon
is scolloped with hills. They roll grandly, carrying
huge bowlders up to the sky-line as if they were
bubbles, and tossing the hemlocks and pines, the
beeches and maples, as if they were lily leaves on
stormy water. Otsego county has pleasant memories
to tens of thousands. To " H. and E. Phinney, Cooperstown," the child-world has been indebted for small
parcels of happiness, — those blessed little primers,
filled with pictures of birds and beasts and good boys
and angelic girls. Think of happiness, "price one
cent!" The writer has a little menagerie, to-day, in
a blue paper cover, bearing the imprint of the Cooperstown firm, that was purchased with a Spanish
sixpence that had been bitten to test it, and lost in
the street and trodden on, and carried in a buckskin
purse and a red morocco pocket-book, and knotted
up in a bandana handkerchief, and paid out for candy
and blackberries and jewsharps; but it never bought
quite so much perfect delight as when it was ex-
changed for H. and E. Phinney's " Book of Beasts
and Birds," and it remains to-day a precious souvenir
of a ruder, simpler time.

Many of the descendants of them that *ticked* their
way into the county with an axe — the woodman's
clock — yet remain among the pleasant hills, and the
blood of the old stock yet courses in the veins of

many stalwart men and pleasant women. After dark,
one night, a wagon-load of cousins climbed rocky
hills, and drove through a ravine black as a wolf's
mouth, and wound up to the summit of the hill.
where, in a spacious home, dwell a pair that pull
down the steelyards at about four hundred pounds;
the house lively with three generations, and there
might easily be four without working a miracle. A
hearty welcome and — feather-beds, fat as if they had
been direct importations from Amsterdam or Rot-
terdam or Potsdam, or some other profane region,
awaited us. A great wavy farm lay around us, eighty
acres of meadow, and regiments of corn, and a sea of
pasture. The milk of two hundred cows is struck
off into cheese, and dated like medallions. The curd
squeaks in your teeth as it did forty years ago, when
they made cheeses about as big as a dinner-plate.
Spring water comes down from the hills of its own
accord, and runs into the house, the barn, everywhere.
The breakfast-table is broad and long and laden. You
think the prayer for "our daily bread" means far
more than you ever dreamed it did, when you see
how the sections disappear by the loaf. The hills
are a hungry place. They talk at breakfast of the
owls they heard last night, of the hundred turkeys
killed by foxes on the farm this summer. It is a
new world. Breakfast over, the family scatter like a
bell-mouthed musket. A boy is driving away a flock
of geese. A dog is taking the cows to pasture. The
mower begins to tick like a gigantic locust in the

hill-meadow. The girls are busy with the great white sea in the cheese factory.

There is a spot, just over the ridge, you hasten to see. It is "a city set on a hill, that cannot be hid"— the silent acres where "the rude forefathers of the hamlet sleep." Near it stands the "Taylor Hill Meeting-House," with a rusty "1822" served up on a wooden platter in the gable,— a house without spire or belfry, and unchanged since the day of dedication, when preachers rejoiced and thanked God, who joined the church triumphant many a long year ago, and men and women sang Old Hundred and Coronation who have learned the New Song. The church has neither pastor nor people. The front door is locked with a stick of stove-wood. You open it and enter the simple sanctuary. On that raised seat along the wall sat the singers — the leader a gray-haired deacon who pitched the tune for forty years. Girls, wives, grandmothers, dead. And there is the pulpit, like the half of an old-fashioned wine-glass fastened against the wall. Two little flights of stairs, straight as "the narrow way," lead up to it. If Elder Bennett ever stood in it, he must have looked like an oak with its foot in a door-yard vase. You enter the little Zion's look-out. On the narrow ledge, guiltless of trimming as a wooden bread-tray, lies the Bible. Like the church, it bears the date of 1822. The bare board seat is as it was in the days of the fathers.

You remember in childhood seeing the little old preacher, Elder Stephen Taylor, who said goin' and comin' and praisin'—but what matters a worthless "g" or so?—stand in that pulpit and preach. It was a sermon, as you recall it now, full of good sense and pure doctrine, and quaint, apt illustration, and decided power. You remember how earnest he became, and how his bald head grew red like "the old man eloquent's" in Congress, as he made for some blundering "gentleman from" somewhere, and pelted him with facts and dates, and chapter and verse, as if they were so many cobble-stones. One of his illustrations you will never forget. He was talking of living "above the world," and he said: "Haven't you seen, my brethren, an eagle when attacked by a flock of little birds, any one of which he could have killed with a stroke of his talon or a blow of his beak? But they are too many for him. They dart up beneath him and vex him. They pounce upon him from above. They scream around his head and bewilder him. He sits upon the tall hemlock as long as he can, and then spreads his great wings. Does he fly down and hide in the bush? Does he waste his strength in attempting to fight an enemy that he cannot number? Oh, no, dear friends, he gives a sweep or two, and up he goes above the hills and the trees. The flock of little birds struggle up after him, but higher and higher he rises into clearer, thinner air; he leaves his busy enemies one after

another. They weary of wing, and sink panting back
to their native woods again. He is alone in the sky;
he is too high to cast a shadow. That eagle, brethren
and sisters, is the human soul, and those little birds
are the sins and temptations that vex us. Never
tarry to fight them. Never think to destroy them,
but just put forth the strength that God gives you
to rise above them all, and so you shall be nearer to
heaven and God. This is bein', as the poet says,
'while in, above the world!'"

The years that are gone throng in at the open
door. You descend from the pulpit, and take a parting look at the old church. On that cross-beam is
the wreck of a bird's nest. Not so widely scattered
is the brood she hovered over as they who once
gathered within these walls. You pass thoughtfully
out into the sunshine, and stand in the shade of the
old church. What is this that grows so rank, and
rattles its ripened sprigs in the morning wind? The
air is sweet with its aromatic breath. It is caraway!
In the days that are gone the congregation brought
their luncheon in summer-time, and sat in the shadow
of the wall between sermons and talked and ate. The
mothers and the girls brought their inevitable clusters of caraway, and seeds were scattered here, and
have sprung up self-sown year after year, "even until
this day." What a sermon upon human life is this!
The caraway remains, but the fingers that strewed it
are nerveless with age, or have forgotten their cunning altogether.

They propose to repair and modernize the old meeting-house, but let them not lay desecrating hands upon
the pulpit. It is as quaint as one of old Herrick's
poems. Let them carpet and cushion and stain and
grain pew and aisle as they will; but farther than
renewing the simple coat of white, let them not touch
that queer little watchman's box for the sentry of the
Lord.

A HEALTH AT BRIDGEWATER.

We have been riding to-day on the heavy swells
of Herkimer and Otsego. The streams through all
the region have an errand and a voice as they run
along their rough McAdams. Every one of them
is as busy as a haymaker. You cross the Unadilla
—as pretty a name for a girl as it is for a river—
fringed with willows that are forever looking at themselves in the glancing water, as if some gigantic naiad
had stitched the bank with double willows and left
the foliage waving free in the water and the air.
" The daughters of Judah " could not have hung their
harps in a prettier place. You go through the old
village of Bridgewater, that has grown like a candle
—less as it grows older; busier, if not bigger, forty
years ago than it is to-day. Bridgewater has a memory.

Many a year ago one of the dead presidents of
Madison University was a student at Hamilton Col-
lege. He had just been graduated. He had taken
the valedictory. He was on his way to his hill-top
home in Edmeston, and he halted at Bridgewater for

dinner. There were with him the girl he was going to marry, her brother, and a young sister of his own. I must lay that clod of a word upon them all to-day. I must say they are dead. At that dinner the young student, as was the fashion sixty years ago, called for a bottle of wine, and filled the glasses, and stood up and drank to the days to come. That was fifty-six years ago, and all the future they were thinking of as they drank has slipped silently and solemnly into the past. A son of the student and the girl halted a moment to-day in front of the old tavern where they met, and this world looked very narrow and very perishable indeed — just an isthmus covered with grass and roughened with many graves.

7*

CHAPTER XX.

JAW.

SAMSON was the most eloquent man of ancient times. He overwhelmed his Philistine audience with jaw, albeit it was the jaw of an ass. Why not? Balaam's beast saw what his master could not discern. He had an angelic vision, and spoke right out. Jaws go in pairs, as Noah's menagerie went into the ark, but it is only the under-jaw that has a character in all creatures but the shark. As for him, that compound adjustment of levers bringing the two rows of cutlery together and setting them wide like the blades of a pair of shears, gives his countenance an open expression that is winning if not amiable.

I once visited a rolling-mill where iron runs about like quicksilver, and railroad bars,—a lift for four knotty-armed men,— glide between the rollers, and thin out as they glide, as smoothly as satin ribbons run over a shop-girl's forefinger. I happened there when a row of boarders, chuckle-headed like young robins, were eating a lunch of cold iron, and snipping off the ponderous bars that were fed to them as easily and noiselessly as a rabbit nips a clover blossom. It was an exhibition of jaw that Samson would have enjoyed.

When a man's head slopes up to the ridge of self-esteem, and then tumbles abruptly down behind, you know he is a man given to reflection,— in a looking-glass; that he has the grace of charity,— for himself; and you envy him a little. But you do not quite know a man until you have measured his lower jaw. When it retreats meekly away, as if it had some notion of slipping down through his cravat into his bosom, you expect to hear him apologizing for his existence. He came into the world with a snaffle-bit in his mouth that holds him back by the jaw, and never slips out. What can we do for a horse that neither pulls by the bit nor draws by the traces?

But when that jaw juts squarely and boldly out like a promontory, and closes upon its neighbor like a vise, as much as to say, "Bring on your walnuts if they want cracking," he has what is called grip in a bulldog, and tenacity in a general. The only way to coax him is to kill him. You have seen a man with such an osseous formation. It took a small lime-kiln to make it. Like the antlers of an elk, it is the most wonderful part of him. Moreover, his superciliary arches are very much arched indeed, and he has a way of lifting the fringe of eyebrow at times that provokes the suspicion that he can slip his scalp off back over his head like a nightcap, if he tries. Then exactly over the eyes, that look as if they were not fast colors, and had been washed in two waters, and exactly over the arches that are nearly sharp enough to be Gothic, and halfway up the slope, rest his spectacles, like a couple of dormer-windows. It is a sort of two-story face, with two rows of windows in it. Then his long hair flows away behind his ears, and rolls down the nape of his neck and ripples over his coat-collar in a kind of John-in-the-wilderness way. This is the sort of front he presents when anybody opposes him. His voice has a twang to it, and twangs prolonged make whines. It has a quaver likewise. He has inherited Samson's own weapon, and with it he sets the doctrine of "ruling majorities" at defiance. He resembles the son of Manoah in two ways: he treats opposing brethren as if they were so many Philistines, and when they are too much for him he bows himself upon the pillars, if so be he may bring down the temple in which he cannot reign.

But the most aggravating thing is yet to be told. Having applied the purchase of that jaw to a question, and held on as vicious as a vise to his own opinion, and worried people until they give in from sheer exhaustion, this man will rise up and bring his two hands together at the finger-tips like a V, and raise his voice and his eyebrows, and extol the beauty of harmony, and say, "Behold, how good and how pleasant a thing it is for brethren to dwell together in unity," when he never agreed with anybody in all his life! Poor Philistines! Jawed to death, and then congratulated upon the disaster.

This man is no fiction, neither is he a stranger. He is in church and state and social life. If on a jury, prayers for the hapless eleven are in order. If leading an army, he pays the highest price demanded for a victory, and never counts the cost. You can pick him out as you could Samson in the temple, for he is the man with the jawbone. There is nothing like an appropriate text when such men let go their hold: "With the jawbone of an ass, heaps upon heaps, with the jawbone of an ass have I slain a thousand men."

CHAPTER XXI.

JUST AND GENEROUS.

THE OLD GUARD.

THERE he paces, to and fro, his red signal of danger furled under his arm. He encounters water in every form. Rain, snow, sleet, hail, fog and steam. He is blown upon by thirty-two winds. Fire tries him summers, and frost takes him in hand winters — and in foot, too, for that matter — but he never flinches. How many men, women and children he has saved from mutilation and death; how many horses from the hands of the knacker, and how many vehicles from the fate of kindling-wood, nobody knows; but then I should like his roll of achievements better than the soldier's who had killed four times as many. He has seen millions of people go by, and cattle from a thousand hills, and there he stands as faithful as a light-house. But he cannot last forever. Some day he must surrender the little red flag. He has been the company's servant about as long as Jacob served to get Rachel. The law of his life is duty. He knows engines by their talk, and freight by its number. He never stole a rod of railroad, or pocketed a switch. But will the great corporation ever put him upon the retired list, and pension him? And yet some

people seem to think well of faithfulness, and several
eulogies in prose and verse have been pronounced
upon honesty by men who would "bear watching"
themselves.

STEALING.

Honesty is a respectable virtue, but it is prodigious-
ly homely. If a man practices it but little, he praises
it a great deal, and so does his duty by it as a sort
of poor relation. Agur was afraid to be poor, and
he did not dare to be rich. He feared he should
swear in the one case and steal in the other. He
was a timid man, was Agur. People have grown
braver since his time. There are several courageous
men in Washington. Now and then there is a lion
among them, and that's what he does. Lie on and
steal on go in couples. It is a horrible pun, but it
is good enough for the subject. If Agur had been
an Indian, and his prayer had been answered, some
of them would have made off with the answer and
left him to pray again. They would have made a
sort of trap of him, to catch answers for them to
steal! Stealing is never respectable unless it is atrocious. When the depredation is so large that twenty
per cent of it will establish his innocence, the man
is a success. Nearly everybody steals something, even
if it is only a march or a glance. What a choir it
would be, if all who could sing it with the spirit,
should join in on the first half line of that familiar
hymn, and stop definitely where it is dangerous to
halt a second:

"I love to steal!"

FAIRS.

The average fair for the sale of worthless articles for noble causes is a place where you are robbed by your own consent, and smiled on by the banditti. You pay a dollar for a pen-wiper, not because a young Kickapoo lacks a blanket, or the pulpit a cushion, but because the lady who halts you in the highway of Vanity Fair has invested a dime in it, and challenges you to make it a dollar, or ——. Well, you "stand and deliver." Somebody gives ten cents in the disguise of a woolen heart, to be pounced upon by steel pens, as that old Greek's was by vultures, and asks you to give ninety. This is the unpopular side of the question, but I submit that I have not left the subject. Why should a fair do for a good sake what an honorable merchant could not do for any sake? Is it fair?

I met a suitable motive for a small fair last Sunday. It was a boy that looked as if his clothes had been torn to pieces by tigers in the interest of tailors out of business. They were so thoroughly ventilated· that their natural home was the rag-bag, and yet he contrived to keep them flapping about him as a sleight-of-hand fellow keeps a half dozen balls going up and coming down and never touching ground. He was barefooted, and his hair grew out of the chinks in his hat. That was his best suit, except the tights he was born in. Whenever a well-dressed lad came within contrasting distance, his tattered decency went into a more dismal eclipse than ever. Now, *he* wants a fair, and there are more of him, and girls to match. Suppose Dorcas should make garments and have a fair, and smile people into buying at honest prices, and then give tatterdemalion the Sunday suit and the new frock, and be rewarded by tatterdemalion's wonder and delight, and have the profits besides, for the aisle carpet, the pulpit cushion, or "India's coral strand." And then you have given the boy a *moral* jog, as well as a braided jacket, for anybody is apt to behave better in good clothes. There is many a man who cannot conduct himself like a christian simply because he is dressed like a beggar.

THE ART OF GIVING.

The Golden Rule is a section of "the higher law." It requires more than a spirit of obedience to obey it. "Do unto others as ye would they should do unto you." That is all of it — easily read, but not easily done. It implies the possession of some imagination, but there are men who are not proprietors of a particle. To step out of yourself and be somebody else, think the whole matter over, and then step quietly back again — all this is involved in it. But did you ever hear a man thank the Lord for his imagination, or pray for a little more? He sometimes names the dinner he is about to eat, but he gives imagination the go-by. He has no idea that he needs any, and associates it with short lines that trot, amble or gallop, as the gait happens to be — short lines, with a capital letter at one end, and a capital jingle at the other,

8

tricked out, as it were, with "bells on their toes."
It is a costly rule, and therefore golden. It costs a
thoughtful self-sacrifice, for which nobody will com-
mend you. Now a just or a generous act committed
in a moment of enthusiasm, when a man shies a plump
pocket-book at an object, in a sort of Fourth-of-July
fervor, is a very different thing from that same act
performed after deliberate premeditation. It means
more, for it is significant of the man. The one is a
principle, the other an impulse. Generosity is a contagious disease, and is always most violent in great
crowds. Men have thus won, in the heat of the moment, the reputation of being munificent, who directly
set about cheating somebody to supply the deficiency.

THE USES OF IMAGINATION.

Most men lack imagination. You never saw a
person yet who did not volunteer the information,
that should he come into a liberal fortune, of which
there was no probability, he would give you at least
ten per cent. out of hand,— ten thousand on a hundred thousand, and if a million, then the cool hundred!
And you try to believe he would do it, and you call
him a generous fellow, and he returns the compliment
when, in like manner, you bestow a few thousands
upon *him*. But such men have no imagination. They
cannot put themselves in the rich man's place, or if at
all, so badly damaged in the transportation that they
do not know themselves when they get there. Be-
nevolence is an easy virtue, but beneficence is quite
another thing.

Giving "blesses him that gives and him that takes" is Shakespeare, but not absolute truth. If the gift costs the giver a temporary privation or an extra effort; if he *accompanies* the gift and sees it actually appropriated, and the comfort and gratitude and happiness it brings; or if he has imagination enough to follow it to its destination, and see with his eyes shut all he would see if actually present, then indeed the act "blesses him that gives and him that takes." The art of giving is one of the fine arts, and not well understood. You have met the lady who embroiders beautiful tidies for the poor, when they all sit upon stools, and elegant little cloaks for children who have nothing to wear when they get them. It resembles the thoughtful kindness of her who sends a tailor's goose for their Christmas dinner, or skates and a buffalo-robe to a Polynesian.

It is a standing wonder that murderers on execution eve sleep soundly, and that, in most instances, they go to their death with unfaltering and sometimes unassisted steps. They are like Pope's lamb in one thing:

> "The lamb thy riot dooms to bleed to-day,
> Had he thy reason, would he skip and play!"

It is a lack of sense in the lamb, and of imagination in the criminal. He never mentally rehearses the catastrophe or the crime, and thinks deliberately through the terrible details. If he did, and when he does, his strength always departs from him. Eugene Aram was a man of imagination. He committed the murder over and over, and death to him was a comfort.

The woman that always sees things with her eyes shut will take a table laden with flowers, and *see* the room decorated with them without touching a bud; and then, before you know it, make the apartment a beautiful picture. So with furniture and adornings. Tumble the whole into the middle of the floor, and she will *see* them all out of chaos into a fitness of position that could not be improved with a month's thinking, and not lay a hand on them at all. It is not taste alone that inspires her. It is imagination also.

There are other women who keep things revolving like the bits of broken glass in a kaleidoscope. Beds, bureaus, chairs and mirrors go round and round like the broom in the riddle, though they do not "pop behind the door," but it would not matter if they did. They are the women that put china cats on the mantlepiece face to face, and lay the show-books like spokes of wheels on the center-table, and back every chair up squarely against the wall, and put one ostrich feather over the looking-glass so, ∕, and another ostrich feather over the looking-glass so, ∖, that the combined effect may be thus, ✕, and so balance everything that the room resembles a donkey between two panniers, or a country doctor's saddle-bags, or any other thing that is distressingly symmetrical. These are the people who want everything to "*compare*," whatever that may mean.

CHAPTER XXII.

STITCHING LANDSCAPES.

DISTANCE, with nothing swift to conquer it, renders the impressive grouping of geographical facts almost impossible. The world lies about in loose leaves. We pick up one here and there, but it is only when the locomotive whips through the miles like a cambric needle along a hem, and stitches those leaves together in a book we can have at once under our eyes, that such facts grow eloquent. Take, some spring day, at Chicago, an express needle on the Lake Shore and Michigan Southern, which is the locomotive. You cling to the thread, which is the train, and within twenty hours you may see men plowing the fields for corn, planting corn, hoeing corn, the three eras in the work grouped upon one illustrated page. You can see lilacs in leaf, lilacs in bud, lilacs in blow, as you cross line after line of longitude as a boy ticks with a stick along the slats of a picket fence. You feel as if you were reading a chapter of prophecy backward.

Those September days, broad, bright and round — the weather that "makes corn," as farmers say — I came east over the New York Central. It was

hot and dusty along the track, but the world was
not dusty, and the green fields and woods looked
cool. The most African and smothering thing I saw
was a man riding upon the yellow road that danced
up and down with the heat, in a "devil's-hornpipe"
sort of way, perched on a load of fleeces; the suggestion of woolen clothes, oily wool and muttonish
odor all simmering together, with a red-faced man
in a narrow hat-brim, like a house without a cornice,
frying in the middle of the mess, made thoughts as
hot as a canal-boat kitchen in dog-days. Association
mercifully helps you in such a case, and you think
of ice tinkling in tumblers, and cool nooks in the
woods, and feel refreshed. I glanced out of the window after a look at that man mounted upon sheep's
jackets, saw a girl under a willow by a brookside,
with her white feet dangling in the running water
and the shadows falling cool upon her, and I was
comforted.

The next minute a strong peppermint breeze blew
into the window. The fields, ridged with rolls of
green, showed the route of the mowers, and a pep-
permint-still threw off its fragrant volumes that sweetened the air laden with coal smoke, and was far fresher
than cologne. The oil, which is a staple of several
sections of western New York — Lyons is one of them
— is only gold in disguise, and meets a ready European
sale. Mint farming seems to me pleasant, though less
emotional than onion-raising, and kinder to the spinal
column.

Writing of Lyons: "the Lady of Lyons" came on board — she and two friends. They may not be residents of that excellent town. They were of the species called chatterers. Taking seats in front and rear of an inoffensive and modest man, they fairly surrounded him, and began to talk loud and sharp as a driver's horn. They seemed to look directly at him as they faced about, but their talk shot by him, just missing now his right ear and now his left. Then the volley would be returned, and take him in the back. Then the third lioness, or what not, took diagonal aim and grazed his nose. It was a triangular voluble duel. The poor man was bewildered. At first he thought they meant *him*, and he looked this way and that, as the words flew like shuttle-cocks, but he soon discovered that he had gotten into a rook's nest. And so they continued talking around him, over him, through him, making him of no more account than a gate-post. Chatterers are many. They are not liable to consumption, neither are the bellows of blacksmiths. They are not readers of Shakespeare. They do not know that a gentle voice is "an excellent thing in woman." Their answers are not of Job's sort that "turneth away wrath."

NICKNAMES.

When people make books and quote Shakespeare, let them not abridge the poacher's name, and end such a passage as "The quality of mercy is not strained" with *Shak.* Think of a pair of sentences like this: "Now is the winter of our discontent made glorious summer! *Shak!*" Why not quote the author of "The Task" as *Cow*, or a line from Titsworth as *Tit*, or the poet of Amesbury as *Whit?* If the writer has left himself no room for anything but a nickname, let him leave it to the wits of his readers to ascertain whether "my name is Norval on the Grampian hills," or anywhere else.

There is such a miserable monotony of names given to children, that when there is a spark of originality it is as pleasant as a ray of light in a dull place. One of the best I know of is a composite, manufactured for a daughter, by an old resident of Gilboa, Schoharie county, New York. It was a Shakespearean christening. The father made all his naming preparations for a boy. Such things are not safe, however. The name he had ready for the stranger was Romeo. The proposed owner arrived. To be sure, it came within one of being a boy, but it was a girl! The father was not to be balked, so he never went out of the play of Romeo and Juliet at all, but he took that classic couple and he blended a word, and he called the little blunder *Romiette,* and she bears the name "even until this day."

We pass the Montezuma Marshes, and the harvest of rushes in tall, narrow-waisted bundles, and remember the rush-bottomed chairs and the rush-lights of the old days, and them that lighted the one and sat upon the other. They were the salt of the earth; and almost before we were done thinking of them,

the wooden parallelograms of pans, with the salt showing white in the sun, were at right of us and left of
us, as we passed the great Salt Licks of New York.

Out of Syracuse, after taking a stitch under the
canal through that eyelet-hole of a tunnel, we whipped
fifty-four miles across country after one of those tem-
perate engines that drink only twice or so in a hundred
miles, to the modern Utica, that is not "pent-up"
except as the president of the New York Central has
fenced a piece of it. Then keeping company with the
Mohawk, we fly by a million or two of wild brooms,
the clean and yellow plumage of the broom-corn
sweeping the sun-bright air, that shall by-and-by be
girded into besoms for kitchen floors and whisks for
garments, and be soiled and worn out in less time
than it took them to grow. Those acres of Mohawk
levels bear all the poetry there is about "Buy a
Broom!" Then the flat Mohawk gets up a little at
its old battle-place, Little Falls, where it had, some
day, a desperate fight with rocks, that came finally
off the worse for wear.

At Schenectady the cars are reinforced by a crowd
of human miscellany. Some Dutchmen, built like
the churns of their foremothers, broad at the base
and tapering out at the top; some specimens of the
tribe of Saratoga accompanying the trunks they had
been living in; some school-girls loaded with log-
chains in ebony and gold, just to help the attraction
of gravitation a little; last and worst, the man and
woman that open the window ahead of you, and let

in upon you the storm of smoke, cinders and dust, while they escape the tempest and are comfortable. You shade your eyes with your hand. You cease to see the bright world going the other way. You catch a cinder in your ear. You breathe smoke. You are a dirt-eater. At last an angel of a cinder gets into that woman's eye, and she weeps for the cinder if not for the sin. Down comes the window, and you betake yourself to breathing a few cubic feet of atmospheric air, damaged, to be sure, but then no ashman would pay as much for it as he might for the article you had just done with.

The train stitches a few of the streets of Albany together,—Albany, where, according to the old chronicler, the inhabitants once stood "with their gable-ends to the street," and we found the Hudson River train in harness awaiting us. The River trains always remind me of blooded horses, rather lean and not well groomed. Compared with their western kindred they are dusty and plebeian-looking things, but they can make time. I like all brakemen, especially *air*-brakemen. They are live brakemen on the Hudson, but they fail in articulation. Their words are like the tails of the Manx cats—all brought to premature ends. One of them opened the car door before the wheels had done rumbling, and said, "*Alas*, poor!" In a few minutes he opened it again, and flung through the crack, "*Yor*ick!" And what he said in the two spasms was straight from Hamlet, "Alas, poor Yorick!" Consulting my guide, I found that

"Alas, poor" was brakemanese for Castleton, and that "Yorick" meant Schodack. He had a way, too, when a name was too long, of catching it in the door and making an insect of it. Thus he gave "Livingston" a vicious pinch thus: | Liviston! | "Liviston!" It was a cheap way of getting at it, and saved breath, but then nobody but a scholar could tell what he meant.

Hudson could not have left his name to a finer thing than that splendid river. There it lay glassy in the sun, cities and villages sitting upon the banks to watch it; mountains in blue cloaks keeping everlasting ward; steamers plying in their direct fashion to and fro; winged craft zigzagging up the river and feeling for wind with slanting canvas palms, or grasping the breeze with a square hold as they swept down toward New York; walls, battlements, towers, that no man builded. Talk of "sermons in stones." O Shakespeare!—but what are your lithoidal preachers to the shrieking dervishes of traffic they have made of cliff and rock all along the river? "Plantation Bitters—S. T. 1860 X!" "Pills!" "Powders!" "Ready Relief!" cry out at you in great letters on every side. They are worse than the Hebrew highwaymen of the old Bowery; worse than Italian bandits. They make a terror of the landscape. But the worst and most impudent of all are those huge, bilious, yellow letters basking on the rocks like rattlesnakes in the sun, within sight of the cars,—"GARGLING OIL!" Is it poison? Will it strangle the proprietor? Will twelve bottles kill him scientifically, and make a sardine of him? It is worth trying, and if successful, let the rocky faces of nature along the Hudson be washed clean of the oleaginous defilement. One of that man's grandfathers must have been a banker in the Temple when that writ of ejectment was served. "Gargling Oil," indeed!

CHAPTER XXIII.

THE COUNTRY BALL-ROOM.

WAS there a troop of strolling players? That ball-room was the scene of their histrionic achievements. Did old Braham, the sweet singer of English ballads,—who, as the frogs piped through the reigns of all the Pharaohs, sang through the reigns of several British lions, not to say lionesses, and then at seventy had a voice as flexible as a girl's,—did he give them an evening of Island melody till the nightingales and the larks seemed singing at once? That ball-room was the music-box for the minstrelsy. One day there came a hungry-looking man,—he *came* from Hungary,—and brought a sort of harp with him, out of whose strings he pulled the battle of Waterloo; guns and groans, battle-cheer and rallying cry, drums and bugles, wailing and sobbing, dirge and anthem, and then, last and best, the song of peace. I do not remember his name, and could not spell it if I did, but he was a wonderful artist, and he stood at one end of the low-ceiled ball-room, and shut his eyes and touched those strings and bent a listening ear, as if he had never heard it before in his life, and we all sat in rows within range of the battle of Waterloo!

181

You should have seen that ball-room on a Fourth of July night, when it was trimmed with asparagus, fresh flowers, and a national flag, and lighted with lamps whose oil came "round the Horn" from the Pacific; when the "grand marshal of the day," and general of militia likewise, led off the dance, a double-handful of gold bullion shining upon his shoulders, and the fringed ends of his sash of crimson silk falling to his knee; when men in blue coats with taper tails and gilded buttons, and dames in caps that flared like full-blown hollyhocks, moved through the graceful measure of the minuet with the coupee, the high step and the balance, amid an atmosphere of lavender, cologne and lamp-smoke; when the air was dizzy with Virginia reels, and as full of "Money Musk" as a Russian lady's handkerchief, and everything was aswing with contra-dances and gay with quadrilles. Not a bearded face among the men, though there was but one barber in the village, and *he* shaved notes and never left a whisker!

Writing of the general: the glitter and tinsel of war's livery is not altogether like Goldsmith's broken china, "kept for show," and it lessens the vanity of the thing a little when we think what the epaulet was really for,—not the modern badge with its modest hint of rank, that would not turn the thrust of a vicious musquito, but the old-fashioned yellow-ringleted shoulder-crest, a sort of mop without a handle, that could dull the downward stroke of sword or saber, and save an arm sometimes. So with the sash. Un-

wound from the waist of the wounded owner, the
elastic web of silk lengthened and widened, and there
you had the hammock whereon the soldier could be
borne away.

Then you recall some other night when, in cutters
by twos, in sleighs by clusters, the young men and
maidens from the country round about, thronged in
for a dance to the old ball-room, and what a medley
it was of morocco shoes, "pumps," red, white and
blue, cheeks, dresses and ribbons, palpitation, poma-
tum, peppermint, and happiness, as bright as a bed of
tulips. And weddings came of the dancings, and
they paired off for the long promenade. And the
names of some of them are on gray slabs of stone,
and some are forgotten altogether. Did you ever see
a rainbow die? — the sort of architecture that must be
repaired every second, or it will crumble into atoms
of colorless rain? And so the drops one by one fall
into their places, the arch changing each instant and
always the same, until the rain comes slow and the
tints grow faint and the bow goes out, and the cloud
is as bare as if God had never put a seal to the Cove-

AN OLD-FASHIONED "FOURTH."

The tavern dining-room on that old Fourth was
the scene of high festivity. The roast pig, with a
sprig of parsley in his mouth, graced the head of the
board. He was as much a belonging of "the day we
celebrate" as the inedible poultry of the flag. It was

pig and patriotism. Before that pig sat the president of the day, blossomed out, as to his broad bosom with snowy ruffles, in vest of buff and coat of blue, and his legs being under the table his pantaloons are out of sight. On either hand is an old soldier of the Revolution, as genuine as a flint-lock : somebody who had seen Washington, and was a captain; somebody who had fought at Bennington, and was a private. And after a while came the stately old toasts, unchangeable as the Book of Genesis, that were drank to the President and the People, the Army, the Navy, the old Soldiers, the Ladies, and the Day. Then they all stood up, and drank in silence to the Dead. After the immemorial thirteen, they toasted each other and "the rest of mankind," and what with the heat of the day, the dinner and the toasting, they grew warm, while the anvil in the street grew hot, and a gun that had bellowed at Sacket's Harbor gave tongue, and the air was full of smoke and glory and Seventy-Six, — Seventy-Six, that had not then sunk so far below the horizon that the twilight splendors of the first Fourth of July that was thought worth mentioning, were not refracted still. Possibly that dinner was fifty cents. Probably it was free. Surely it was grand!

Out in front of the door was a grizzly drummer with his drum, who had beaten the long roll somewhere, because Baron Steuben or General Stark — Molly's husband — told him to; and a fifer to match, who whistled away like a blackbird in a hedge, and the boys kept step to the measure, and everybody marked time with head or toe or cane, and so all mentally marched back fifty years, when the music meant business. But the fife was given to grand-children for a plaything, and Time slashed a hole in the drum with a careless cut of his scythe, and the mice gnawed off the snare, and there are two tablets, each with a stone willow thereon, and both tablets cry out with one voice: "A Patriot of the Revolution." *Sic transit gloria mundi ad immortalitatem* —So passes the glory of the world to immortality.

The Fourth of July has worn on into the deep night. The fifth will soon dawn. The guests are gone. The lights are out. The old inn is silent as an empty church. And so I say to the memory of the old day, "Out! brief candle!"

THE FLAG REMEMBERED.

Forty years ago flags were fewer, and so, to be sure, were folks. The pagans that dwelt in villages seldom saw any except at "General Training" and on the Fourth of July, and on those occasions their name was not legion. Not then, as now, did each omnibus horse sport a little flag between his ears upon gala days. It used to be that a boy's first sight of the glorious standard almost took his breath away. A boy's tenth-wave passion is for martial "pomp and circumstance," provided he has ever seen any. Boys are monkeys. So much for Darwin!

Your first sword was forged from a shingle and

8*

tipped with the blood of the belligerent strawberry. Your first flag was made of a yard square of cotton cloth, that mayhap had helped to do duty upon a trundle-bed, and was hemmed by a mother's fingers. Upon it was tethered with needle and thread an eagle of blue broadcloth. That eagle was hatched by the same loving hands and the help of a pair of shears. It was a fowl of such proportions as Agassiz would have wondered over. Beside it were thirteen stars of blue upon a cotton-white heaven — all "deeply, darkly, beautifully blue," but just the thing that *should* have been cerulean. It was a defiant flag, for it bleached out the sky and put all the color in bird and stars. A disabled broom furnished the staff, and altogether it was the ensign of no State in the Union but the State of Perfect Happiness. Long ago, the moths devoured the eagle and the mice ate up the flag, and the staff turned into legs for a milking-stool, but the memory and the glory remain "even until this day."

CHAPTER XXIV.

A THANKSGIVING-DAY FLIGHT.

BY invitation I rode hundreds of miles to reach New York, for the sake of flying back to Chicago by the Fast White Mail when such things were. That is all there was of it. Three o'clock Thanksgiving morning found me riding up Broadway to the Grand Central Depot.

The city had fallen asleep in her diamonds the night before, — the careless, magnificent creature! Chains of brilliants and necklaces of light and double rows of jewelry down every street, like double rows of gems along a Persian seam, fairly clothed her with trinkets as with a garment. She is grand when she goes to bed as a princess going to Court. But New York sleeps with one eye open. The mantle of slumber is as short as a Scotch kilt, and the cloak of forgetfulness shrinks to a jacket when she puts it on. Nowhere else in America is a man reduced from an integer to a pitiful vulgar fraction as he is in New York. He sees himself through the other end of the glass; he shrivels like a last year's filbert; he wonders the census-taker cares to reckon him in, the three-ninths of a man that he has become. That feeling of fragmentary humanity and loneliness proves, without the help of mathematics, that a mart has achieved genuine greatness. Boston is Athenian; Baltimore is monumental; Philadelphia is centennial; Chicago is wonderful, but New York is NEW YORK.

"THE WORD GO."

Not a minute too soon, we found the White Mail just ready to leave. It had an unreal, a spectral look in the flicker of the lamps, and so had the white four-in-hand, attached to the ponderous wagon, whence the last of the mail-bags were tumbling into the cars. It was a scene for lamplight and starlight rather than for broad day. Number 84, the engineer in the saddle, was ready to run, and, as the clock marked fifteen minutes past four, the conductor gave the word "go," and we went. The crew had come aboard, the engine had made ready, the driver had taken aim, and the conductor said "fire!" That was how it was. There were four cars, four gallant governors in line,— their Excellencies Hendricks, Fairchild, Beveridge and Buckingham,— brave in their white, orange and gold, blazoned with shielded eagles, and gay to look at as so many waiting lords in the king's livery. Ah! it was a *Jewell* of a train.

And the first thing it did was to plunge ignobly into a hole two miles long, burrow like a gopher, and jar away under the city streets that ribbed it overhead like the bars of a gridiron. And the next thing it did was to dash across Harlem river, and make the switches snap like flint-locks in a skirmish, and set the lamp-posts about as near as a row of wax lights on a mantelpiece, and out it dashed as if bound for a plunge-bath in the Hudson. But it changed its mind in a minute and doubled capes of curves, and thundered under the hills, threw lights on the water, and glimmers on the rock, and glares on the rail. It swung like a cradle and shot like an arrow, and whipped through the tunnels as if it were stitching for life, with Starvation's ivory grin looking in at the door. Figures started out in the flash of the head-light as we rounded a promontory, and slunk back in the darkness like guilty things as we passed. The train ran as light and swift, with its thirty-five tons of mail, as a rejoicing herald that used to run before the king. It cleft the shadows that lay heaped upon the track, as if Night had disrobed, left its clothes upon the rails, and gone into the river to swim; ghosts of precipices and doubles of trees and mantles of mountains. The furnace door played like a fan in a fever. The clouds above the engine turned white and crimson and black every two minutes. It was a medley of sunsets and midnights. It seemed like flying, and had we heard the flap of a pair of wings as big as a mainsail close to our ears, and the Governors had all left the track in a flock and flown, not into the ditch, but over the Palisades or Wolfert's Roost, or the Catskills, or the bridge of Anthony's nose, it would have astonished nobody very much.

We had strung a dozen villages as nimble girls string beads, when day broke and the sun touched up the wavy sky-line of the mountains, and Father Hudson showed himself, icy at the edges like the tips of an old man's ears and fingers in a frosty morning, but traveling seaward as sturdily as Sir Hendrick saw him many a year ago. Now we caught one steamer with the steady see-saw of her walking-beam, and showed her a light pair of heels in three seconds; and now we met another with a brood of barges about her like a hen with a small family of exaggerated Bramahs; and now a pair of schooners wing and wing like a couple of gulls. The villages across the river kept dressing to the right, like a row of school-children ranged for a spelling-match, as we flew. The engine was incessantly giving two little whistles to itself, as it cleft hamlet, highway and hill, and the bell swung like a pendulum with a tongue in it, and we pulled up at Poughkeepsie. The wheels tolled along under the train at the blow of the testing hammers before we fairly halted; five minutes and we were away. It is the most penurious train on the road. It puts eighty minutes into sixteen little packages for its sixteen halts in a thousand miles, and it doles out these five-minute nickels one at a time along the way.

THE FLIGHT.

It was a splendid day. The sun shone like an Easter sun. It was Thanksgiving. And to think that we were making the transit of six States before

men should begin to say, "Yesterday was Thanksgiving;"—that New York, Pennsylvania, Ohio, Indiana, Michigan, Illinois, should slip away beneath
the wheels like a map of sovereignties under a nimble
finger;—that we were gliding through an atmosphere
of five hundred thousand turkeys done to a golden
brown and lying like dead knights in armor, ready
for the glad solemnities of Thanksgiving, and not so
much as a "merry-thought" wherewith to bless our-
selves;—that there we were, chasing a cup of coffee
across the Empire State, telegraphing Utica from Albany and Syracuse from Utica, and catching the slow-
footed Mercurys before they had delivered the mes-
sage;—calling for a drop of Java or Mocha or "peas,
beans and barley O," through a flight of two hundred
miles, as plaintively as agnish Cæsar called for drink
when he was in Spain;—that we were to catch at
Buffalo at last and have our small Thanksgiving;—
that we were doing the twenty-six days' work of the
pioneers in as many hours;—that we were in effect
bringing Chicago to sit by the shore of Lake Erie,
and Buffalo to the banks of the Mohawk, and Utica
for a neighborly gossip with the old city of the Knick-
erbockers at tide-water, setting sober-going watches
in the wrong and making them bear false witness
without lying.

GEOGRAPHY JUMBLED.

The train takes Holland in a trice of hours and
captures the savages in a trice more. It is Spuyten
Duyvil, Yonkers, Sing Sing and no music; it is

Crugers and Peekskill, Fishkill and Catskill; it is
Staatsburg, Rhinebeck, Germantown, Stuyvesant, Batavia and Amsterdam. It flashes by the sturdy Dutchmen a hundred years old, whose rugged walls shed
Revolutionary bullets and flint-headed arrows as ducks
shed rain.

It is Tribes Hill and Oriskany, Oneida, Canastota,
Canaseraga, Chittenango and White Pigeon. And
there's your poor Indian! It takes Rome before it
is done with it, and rattles geography together in a
hopeless jumble in twenty-six hours.

"TRUE AS A DIE."

Did you ever see a woman weave, and watch the
play of the shuttle to and fro through the countless
threads and never a tangle or catch?—to and fro,
here and there, with a swing of the bar? The Hudson River Railroad is a loom mightier and busier.
See the sixty trains out of New York flying hither
and yon and keeping the rails jarring night and day
to the music. See the scores of trains dashing out
of the West. See them pulling into "the piece" all
along the way. These are the threads. Then see
the white shuttle of the Fast Mail,—white that everybody may know it,—flashing to and fro amid the
warp and woof of trains, never colliding or blundering or waiting. New York throws it with a will in
the morning and Chicago sends it back in the evening. Shuttles meet and pass and part with the accuracy of the stars.

There is a point on the New York Central between Batavia and a place-no-place called Croft's. The Mail from New York and the Mail from Chicago, nine hundred and eighty-six miles apart, are due there at the same moment,—nineteen minutes past two p. m. We, westward-bound, are careering at fifty-six miles an hour. We shall strike the point on time. Will our twin from the West be there to meet us? Watches in hand we look ahead. A cloud no bigger than a man's hand. It might be a fleece from Mary's little lamb. It grows, till it is like a ship showing everything that will draw. It is the train! Two seventeen — seventeen and a half'— eighteen — a quarter — half — three-quarters — *nineteen !* The train is here, is there, is gone! We met on the instant. It was an aggregate motion the trains made of one hundred and twelve miles an hour. It was like brushing one palm with the other in the twinkling of an eye. A man may build the great clock of Strasburg that could never make a time-table.

A MILE A MINUTE — HOW IT SEEMS.

Of a truth it is a splendid day! Engine 317, H. S. Shattuck, engineer, awaits us at Buffalo. He is of age on the rail, having been an engineer his twenty-one years. We climb into the howdah, and doesn't 317 shine in her brazen harness, like the near wheel-horse of Phœbus! She has done her mile in fifty-two seconds, and never "turned a hair." The engineer is as quiet as the keeper of a light-house. He

9

is not noisy. Engineers seldom are. He is reticent.
He is not a stage-driver. He is a gunner. He says,
"I use my ears as much as I do my eyes. I hear
every click and clip of engine and train. If there's
a jingle out of place anywhere, I can't *help* hearing
it. Once I could not have heard it had I tried."
He talks one way and looks another. He has his
hand on the iron bridle, his eye on the track, his
heart on the West. He sees the world bearing down
upon him like a ship before a mighty wind. He
brings his engine down to her steady work. The
day is as calm as old Herbert's blessed Sunday, but
the wind blows here in the saddle full fifty miles an
hour. A couple of young hurricanes are following
at the heels of the train. Give them a wide berth,
or they will waltz you in upon the track to the tune
of the devil's hornpipe. We are making a mile in
fifty-nine seconds, fifty-eight seconds, fifty-six seconds,
fifty-four seconds. Sheridan's ride at Read's rhythmic paces from Winchester to glory, "only twenty
miles away," was a Sabbath-day's jog in a decorous
way.

The track sometimes lifts to the edge of the sky,
and it doesn't look as if it were a very heavy grade
to heaven either. The telegraph poles come together
like a V, and fence the track in the distance. The
wires droop and swing and shorten up like clothes-
lines to hang sheet lightning on, if you please! The
great steel S's of curves glitter like silver in the sun.
The bell, shaped like the tall hats we see in pictures

finishing up the Pilgrims that stand freezing round the rock of Plymouth, keeps on the swing, rung by the tireless hand of steam. The engine talks to a crossing, hails a station, screams at a track-man. The little oscillations and petty jolts disappear. The thing runs like a shaft in a polished groove. All minor motions are resolved into the one forward plunge. As the rifle-bullet hurries round and round and out of its spiral hall of steel, so speeds the train. It runs as true as the aim of a dead shot. The steady stillness is suspicious. If you think of it and what it means, it tugs at your nerves and draws them taut as the little string of a violin. It is seventy feet at a clock-tick, eighty feet at a heart-beat, forty miles in forty-three minutes. It means that a minute makes a mile, when it does not mean more. Fifteen minutes late is twelve miles late, and a stern chase is a wild chase.

A MAN HATCHED AND RECONSIDERED.

There's a dot on the track about the size of a Darwinian primal egg. It begins to hatch! It develops legs and arms and feet and head. It is as tall as a pen-holder, a walking-stick, a man. It *is* a man, and the man stands not "upon the order of his going," but goes at once, bolts the track and makes for the fence. We pass him, and behold he shuts up like a telescope and diminishes by swift degrees and rolls back into an egg, a dot, a nothing. The track is clear behind us for all such animalculæ as he. It is as if he had never been hatched at all!

The talk of engineer, fireman, conductor, brakeman, is "speed." Watches are in hand, and mileposts read like a book. No vain girl with a pretty face ever consulted her looking-glass so often as are the time-pieces on the train, and it isn't the hour hand they are after, but the minutes and the seconds. Under the wheels of a fifty-six miler time is ground exceeding small, and it takes a finger as delicate as a second hand to pick it up. Speed has a *bead* on it. It is exhilarating as sparkling Catawba. It quickens pulses and lifts the spirits. It is the very antipodes of death, for the swiftest motion is the intensest life.

We have done our thousand miles between sun and sun, our Thanksgiving-day flight is finished, and we say to ourself, as we leap from the train, with some grateful feeling befitting the day we had spent in flying,

Chicago! and we kept the track!

And what have they all done in the twenty-six hours? Scattered to the four winds, and precisely where they belong, 157,000 papers, 119,420 letters,—276,420 pieces in all, and an average of 9,214 to the man,—the work of thirty-five men in a round day!

Chicago, six fifty-five, twenty-six hours from New York, and a cloudy morning! The waiting trains are in harness. It is Illinois, Iowa, Nebraska, Wisconsin, the Silver State, the Golden State, the Picket Post of Civilization. On rush the tidings. It is Green Bay before bed-time. It is Dubuque before sundown. The old fifty-eight hours from Boston to Burlington are forty-five. The old seven days to San Francisco are fused into a bright new six, and a Sabbath to spare! Where are the people that bade each other good-by, as for a lasting farewell, when the mail was chucked into the boot of the Concord coach at Chicago, and trod upon by the driver and lurched away to Galena for ninety-six hours?

Eloquence may be grand, but this is grander. Poetry may be fine, but this is finer still. War may be glorious, but there is no blood on the white array of the Governors' Train. It has swung through an arc of nine hundred and eighty-five miles. It has traversed twenty cities with an aggregate population of two millions. It has flashed along a great highway bordered with half a million more who are within stone's throw or ear-shot of its lively wheels. It was the pendulum of the new Centennial Clock sweeping six States at a vibration.

CHAPTER XXV.

AMERICA has a lake and a river that are classic.
The one is the Hudson, and the other, Otsego.
If anybody thinks there should be more, let him
make more, and no man shall forbid him. Happily
Washington Irving and Fennimore Cooper were eldest sons, and so heirs to whatever of literary name
and fame was worth inheriting. They had no rivals
and few imitators. They entered into peaceable possession when the world was less troubled with angels
than it now is,— the angels that are incessantly saying
" Write ! "

Born fifty years later, they would have been anach-
ronisms, and might about as well have not been born
at all. The world grows more difficult to be caught
every day of its life, but there is a chance for the
man who is born too soon. The quick world may
overtake him and honor him with a monument,
though it has quite forgotten where he was buried.
That coroners can hold an inquest upon departed
merit, without having a *body* to sit upon, is a blessed
thing for printers and marble-workers and everything
but the departed merit. Few are they who, like Professor Morse, witness the unveiling of their own statues.

In this, Cooper and Irving were alike: both loved England filially — faithfully. The one bestowed upon her his benedictions; the other was as much an Islander as he *could* be in the heart of a continent. Both were insular in their tastes. They would have been contented with an asteroid if they could have taken the choicest of this great lumbering earth with them; if they could have had at command a small marine to carry their manuscripts to the mainland. They were neither sordid nor selfish, but then they did not like to be jostled.

It is not long since Irving's Sketch-Book and Cooper's Leather-Stocking were in everybody's hand, when "everybody" meant less and more than it means now; less, because readers were fewer; more, because the few read as the saints are charged to sing, "with the spirit and the understanding also." How Smith would fare to-day as the author of Irving's Broken Heart, or what publisher would be gracious to Jones, author of Cooper's Pioneers, is a curious inquiry. Whether the *Ledger*, wherein Henry Ward Beecher writes a hay-fever serial, would accept them, or yet any magazine yield them a place with The Luck of Roaring Camp, is not certain. Let us give the men of Lakeside and Riverside the benefit of the doubt.

Among the ways of estimating literary fame are the time-table and long measure. An exemplary dog ordinarily lives longer than a book. Twelve years is a great while in the ephemeral generations of print, and the Methuselahs are rare. A work that can stand

the ravages of a century, and then come up somewhere in a man's path like a fresh flower in the
spring, and brighten his way and gladden his heart,
and with human nature enough in it to live another
hundred, has achieved a fame that men agree to call
immortality,— a sort of infant immortality in swad-
dling bands.

As a rule, a popular writer appears greater and
grander at a thousand miles than he does at your
elbow. He looms. The eagerness of people to subject a favorite to the damaging microscope of daily
observation almost always brings its own punishment
in one idol less and more bits of broken pottery. The
paths of some, to-day, are as rough with them as the
road to Jordan. Death and distance are great illu-
sionists, and many a man owes the glamour of his
fame to one or the other, and for the same reason,—
it keeps him out of sight.

But why these dealings with the dead? Are there
not livelier, fresher themes going? The works of
Irving and Cooper have long since taken their allot-
ted places in the world of letters. Brave in turkey
and gilding they are drawn up in thousands of glittering lines; a little more like Joseph, perhaps, with
the strange king upon the throne who knew him
not; a little more dust upon them, a little oftener,
than there was twenty years ago; but what matters
it? When the fine wines in the cob-webbed bottles
come up from the bin, there is a *brush* with the cork-
screw ready to your hand. The amber, the crimson,

and the golden set themselves aright, and show the drowned sunshine all the same. So, the delicate touch, the apt word, the finished English, the quaint and quiet humor of Irving, are still there. The salty breeze of Cooper's sea-stories has not lost its savor. Natty Bumppo, Leatherstocking, Hawkeye, the Scout, the Pathfinder, the Trapper,— the many-sided man of Otsego,— yet counts five in the roll of manhood.

And this is why. October has a thoughtful way with it. *Pansies* should be born in October. The woods, trying to remember the colored splendors of the going year, have taken fire, and yet are unconsumed. Maple, poplar, beech and ash tell the story, every one in its own way, and thus it is that there are "tongues in trees." With their dying leaves they repeat the marigolds. They suggest the blush-roses. They rehearse the summer-sunsets. October is a good time for a pilgrimage, and I have just made one to Cooperstown. What you can find in a geography or a tourist's guide, or anybody's Field Book of anything, cannot be found here.

Striking out by an unwonted route from Richfield Springs, where people drink disagreeable water and fan themselves all summer, twelve miles to Cooperstown as the crow flies, if he flies straight, you pass little hamlets you never heard of, noted on the map with a fly-speck of a dot, as Cooperstown might have been but for Cooper and his creations. There is something breezy about hills, even when no wind is blowing. They suggest billows.

As long ago as I hid "The Last of the Mohicans" under the fat copy of Virgil spread open before me in school-time,—Virgil, with a blessed *"Ordo"* running down the edge of the text, the clew of the labyrinth to take a fellow through the dove-tail terminations out into English light and Latin sense,— before that, Cooperstown was a Mecca to me,—and not to me only, but to thousands. I fancied it was about a mile from the Celestial Gate, and stored with countless wealth. Thence came the books of birds and beasts, the blessed primers thin as gold leaf and quite as precious,—"price one cent;" "price two cents;" "price six cents." But, ah! the last was magnificence, at the cost of a Spanish sixpence, the scale from a little silver fish that had been mentally taken to pieces ever so often, resolved into cents, reduced to mills, and there they were, all rounded into the small flake from the white mines of Peru! Since then I have spent delighted hours before Audubon's Book of Birds, as it leaned up against the wall like a pier-glass. Had the partridge began to drum, nobody could have wondered. But never did that wondrous mimicry of nature give me half the joy that one of those bits of blue-covered primers did, with the imprint, "H. & E. PHINNEY." And here, a while ago, I was riding into Cooperstown in the October sunshine of a perfect day, and, passing along the street, an ancient landmark of a store caught my eye, and across its front was a wooden sign, like a railway passenger with his ticket in his hat-band, and

the words upon it were familiar as a nursery rhyme.
It was as if somebody you had thought dead full
forty years ago should meet you with the old greeting.
The sign was "in words and letters following, to
wit": H. & E. PHINNEY. The pack of care and
time I had been carrying tumbled off in an instant,
like Christian Pilgrim's knapsack of sin, and again
I was the beatified master of a silver sixpence. *This*
was the place, then, whither the jingling treasures in
the pockets of my blue-striped trousers found their
way, and whence, in the old time, came those thin-
leaved tracts of boyish happiness! The modern stores,
the fine old mansions, the grand hotels, all faded out
like a mirage, and, for the moment, nothing remained
of Cooperstown but the old sign.

We passed an ancient church-yard, where, like lambs
around the door, stood the white tablets of the forefathers. But the slabs leaned hither and thither, as
if they would lay the heavy emphasis of marble *Italics*
upon human forgetfulness. And there lies the dust
of the novelist! The living world has closed around
the disused acre, but I had found the resting-place of
him with whom, many a year ago, by the magic of
his story, I had wandered in the wilderness; who
had halted my heart many a time in hours of mystery
and danger; had quickened it to exultation in the
triumphing right, and inspired me with a love for
American scenery by forest and prairie, by valley and
mountain; with an admiration for American purpose
and prowess everywhere, that have never perished. His

pictures were appeals for things noble and lovely, and of good report. He suggested no evil. He mossed over no wrong. In all English-speaking lands he compelled recognition of the truth that an American could write an American novel, that, owing nothing to the old world, should spring as naturally from the soil as the elms and pines of Otsego. A gay and gilded omnibus rattled by, blazoned with HOTEL FEN-NIMORE. Italics and great capitals,—weeds unrebuked and the pride of life. "So runs the world away!"

The last trace of the old Cooper mansion is obliterated. Fire began it. Innovation completed it. Nothing remains but to sow it with salt. The classic grounds have been virtually slashed with a public street, as a saber-stroke seams and disfigures a noble face, and houses stand about, and look foolishly at each other, as if they were ashamed of it. Even some of the old ancestral trees, they say, have been deemed cumberers of the ground, and have gone up sooty kitchen-chimneys in smoke. Nothing of all this is half so wonderful as where the willing hands were folded, that the spot was not rescued from oblivion; and where the taste had vanished that would have made a Leatherstocking Park, and thronged it with the creations of Cooper's genius; embodied his characters in marble and bronze, civilized, savage and sailor, the red, white and blue of his stories, and deeded it all to the people forever.

Then we crossed a picturesque ravine, and wound along the base of the wooded hills, Otsego's classic water at the left, turned golden wine in the descending sun; and, terrace above terrace, the city of the silent at the right. The very water where the canoes of the wilderness glided with an arrow's silence. The very city where, among the sighing pines, and the flickering shadows blown about upon the ground and spotted with fallen leaves by October winds, Cooper's monument stands forth. It is an eloquent piece of work. Eloquent, not so much in what is graven as in what is left unsaid. No word but COOPER. No name his mother called him by. No date of birth or death. Why *should* there be? In everything that makes true living he is *not* dead. Leatherstocking, in his fringed hunting-suit and frowzy cap,— as classic, every whit, as the robe of the Roman,— his faithful friends, the dog and rifle, bearing company, surmount the shaft. Emblems of Cooper's works by ship and shore emboss the monument with brief biography. The word Otsego had a meaning once, of salutation and honor. The red-man's courtesy is in order to-day, and so let me say, Otsego to Cooper!

Miles of hill and dale lay between us and rest; the sun was going down, and taking one look more at lake and hill and sky and monument I turned silently away. I had come on a pilgrimage to what men call the Dead. Eating salt at no man's table, entering no abode of the living, welcomed by none, I left Cooperstown, and before many miles were made, night fell down upon all the hills.

CHAPTER XXVI.

CHECKS.

THE CONDUCTOR'S CHECK.

WRITING of checks: I was a passenger on the Cincinnati and Sandusky railroad, where the conductor gives no check, but takes your ticket, looks you over for a second and passes on. It is a great comfort all around. It saves you the annoyance of a conductor's feeling about for some place to stick a label, red, white, blue, or yellow as a daisy, as if you were a package of goods consigned to somebody. It always gives me a bit of spiteful satisfaction when the conductor finds a hat without any band, or a band stitched so snugly that he cannot embellish it with a check. It delights me to see him give little *jabs* with his parallelogram of pasteboard around that hat's equator without finding a place to put it, and then irritably hand it to the passenger with a gesture of expostulation.

Did you ever watch a woman look for her check when the conductor demands it? She has no hatband, thank fortune and fashion! but what to do with it is a conundrum. She holds the representative of money paid and miles to ride in her hand a little while. Then, tired of that, she wedges it between her

glove and the palm of her hand; or she puts it in
her portemonnaie or her reticule or her lunch-basket
or her bandbox or her pocket. If very primitive, she
thrusts it in her bosom or knots it up in a corner of
her handkerchief, as old grandmothers used to tie up
their money. Perhaps she gives it to the baby for
amusement, and the youngster plays paper-mill with
half of it. She sticks it in a crack of the window
for security, and it slips down upon the floor. She
steps out into the aisle, adjusts her skirts, and makes
a dip and a plunge under the seat for it. Rescued,
she impales it with a pin upon the side of the car,
and it jars out into her lap in a mile. She catches
it, and gropes for her basket, overturns a sandwich,
two pickles, a stratum of cheese and a doughnut, and
deposits it in the very bottom of the geological forma-
tions. That miserable bit of paper is the most troublesome of all her possessions.

She is glad it is an "Indian gift," that the conductor did not present it to her outright, that he will
relieve her of it in due time, but by-and-by she is
sorry she was glad. There he stands, and he wants
that check. She has forgotten what she did with it!
She nervously examines her portemonnaie, she over-
hauls her reticule, she feels in her glove, her pocket,
her bosom. She wishes the conductor wouldn't watch
her. She could find it quicker if he only wouldn't.
At last she unearths it from the big basket, smelling
of vinegar and cheese and nutcakes, and stained with
a drop of jelly, like "the damned spot" upon the

little hand of Shakespeare's monster, Lady Macbeth, that would not "out," and presents it with a sigh of relief to the impatient official. Nibbled at one end and soiled at the other, he tears it in three pieces, and hastens along; and the woman wonders why upon earth he troubled her to keep it, when he didn't want it himself.

Yonder is a young woman who has traveled. She pins the check upon her shawl the minute she gets it, like an order of nobility, and thinks no more about it. She does not care the pin that holds it whether the conductor ever gets it or not. All the timid women and the elderly women envy her. Here is a man who consigns that check to his tin tobacco-box, and snaps the cover together with a click. Unhappy is he whose check the conductor took from his hatband while he nodded, as even Homer is said to do; taken as was the rib from Adam, but with no hope of a recompense so pleasant as Eve. He wakens with a start, throws up a hand instinctively to his hat, for he knows he has been "in the land of Nod," feels nothing, whips off the castor, and gives it three complete revolutions before he is convinced that the check has utterly gone, and then falls to searching in all his pockets and around the neighborhood, glances suspiciously at its inhabitants to see who took it, gives the hat another hopeless twirl, and then waits helplessly for the conductor that never comes back, and so the passenger escapes safely from the car at his destination, ignorant what became of that check.

THE BANK CHECK.

Of all checks bank checks are the pleasantest. Almost every boy has written out one of them for a million or so, upon the Bank of Nowhere, and put his name to it just to see how it would look. I wonder how a man feels who can fill in a slip of paper with such words and figures, to wit, as "ten thousand dollars — $10,000," and have some paying teller wet his fingers and count them out the minute it is presented. It must be a warming sort of sensation, like a mustard-plaster applied to a cold place. Is that why wealthy men are called "warm"?

Girls never do that. They never write make-believe checks, for they hope to live till somebody pens genuine checks for them, and saves them the trouble and the — expense.

Are you ever made game of by autograph-hunters? Do they come at you with a pen, a pocket-inkstand with a screw cover, and a narrow book containing everybody's name "his mother called him by"? Are you an impecunious poet or a peripatetic lecturer, or something of that sort? If you are, then you have. That putting your signature to *nothing* is a flattering business before twenty-five and a stupid one after two-score. The writer hopes the reader's name is not found in many autograph albums, belaureled, bedoved and beharped on the covers, and gilt-edged, like Orange county butter, because, as a rule, you don't find a name good for much on a bank-check flourishing in an album. Whether or not it is because the

9*

owner is afraid somebody will steal the autograph and put it where "it will do the most good," I cannot tell.

It *must* be pleasant to be able to make a check. It is something like earning the money, and then issuing the currency yourself. I am not quite sure it would not be a luxury to put a dollar into some bank just for the sake of checking it out. But there is always a time in a man's life, and it is not in the beginning of it, when these slips of paper, even with seven figures on them besides the pair for cents, look microscopically worthless, and that is when, in language more current than classic, he is summoned "to pass in his checks"; when the word is "checkmate!" and the end comes. A man has recently gone who could have drawn a check that would have bought Louisiana at its old price, and fenced Rhode Island, and filled a great State with homes for the poor, and founded a great library. He dealt in hot water, boiling water, winged water, all his days, and steamed with unparalleled swiftness to a fortune so stupendous that he reckoned his life not by years, but by millions. He checked out a church and a university as if they had been trifles. But then he was a long time on the track. He bought and sold speed as if it were a commodity, but he could not "make time" himself.

TRUNK CHECKS.

There is a jingle as of dull bells, and a man enters the car, dragging after him a frame hung with geography tumbled to pieces, picked up, graven upon bits of brass, and hung upon leather straps. And the man says, "*Check* y'r baggage!" Your thought climbs a flight of garret stairs somewhere, and stands by a little calfskin trunk with the hair on, and your name lettered with brass nails on the cover, "A. B. C." That was all the check anybody had thirty years ago. Fancy a man — fancy two hundred men — looking for "A. B. C." in a through baggage-car! Put a brass ornament on that home-body of a trunk, and, calf as it is, it will reveal powers of going abroad that are marvelous. It will travel like a thing with brains, in a sort of intelligent manner, from Maine to the Florida reefs, and there you will find it waiting for you, chafed as to its epidermis, weak and jingling of a hinge, perhaps, but then there.

How many men have *themselves* checked through a line of policy, regardless of friends, foes or consequences! Put brazen labels on their heresies and set them going!

BLUE CHECK.

In Ohio I saw a girl in a span-clean checked apron that went around her waist with a string; the old-fashioned sort, made of numberless and undivided checker-boards, with the little blue and white squares alternating with mathematical precision. The sight of that apron would have taken you back to an older wearer of a similar garment, who brought apples from the orchard in it, and white maple-chips from the woodpile, and picked peas in it upon a pinch, and gathered eggs in it from the haymow, and spread it smoothly and decorously over her lap when she sat, and her knitting-work reposed in it; and sometimes a cat, marked like her best Sunday comb, would assay a slumber upon its checkered existence, and be whisked off in a second. You have seen that apron flung over its owner's head like "the knitted cloud" of modern times, when she went to the next neighbor's. That apron has wiped away the tears of your childish sorrow, when they ran down your face, and your clamorous tongue ran out at each corner of your mouth between the sylla-bles of lamentation and licked them in! You see where she laid it when its work was done. You saw where they laid her when *her* work was done. There is a whole system of mnemonics in those blue and white checks.

"CHECK."

So says the reader who has come bravely on to this paragraph, and check it is.

Check!